SNATCH 2&20

A SATIRICAL ROMP THROUGH THE WALL STREET AND SILICON VALLEY SWAMPS

LUKE E. FELLOWS

To my deceased father and ceaseless family.

POST NON-MORTEM

MY FIRST MEMORY in life is getting my diaper changed. As I coo and gurgle, two deliciously pendulous breasts hover in front of me. I grab and nuzzle. "Mamma," I babble.

It is also my first memory after the crash.

You might think that waking up from a coma would be a bit of a downer. It's a reasonable supposition; but I surfaced from a deep dream oxymoronically—both supine and erect. "Sister!" I babbled.

"Get your hands off of me, Mr. Good-e-no," a woman exclaimed in a Staten Island accent guaranteed to deflate my enthusiasm.

"…enough," I offered limply as I unhanded the ample globes and tried to pull myself up on the bed. "Goodenough." I was clearly flailing in response to my first #metoo incident, both literally and figuratively.

I soon realized that my physical efforts were in vain. Though my arms and hands were able to move quite freely, the rest of my body was as rigid as an iron log encased in kryptonite. I felt what I quickly realized was a neck-brace, but had no idea why I couldn't move my legs. Knowing that I could feel them though, or at least my critical upper-central thigh zone, was comforting.

"Enough *already*, more like. Not for nothing, you'd betta watch out," scolded the nurse.

I pretended to be unconscious again, closing my eyes just far enough to look comatose while still getting a dazzling but blurred outline of an unfamiliar world. I had apparently just been propped up, and I could make out the silhouette of a diaper (confirmed by my unfortunately undamaged olfactory organ) being removed from under me. And the rough wipe of a tissue-covered hand corroborated that my backside was just as sensitive as my front.

With a disgusted and exasperated "uchh," the boxy mass of the offended woman cantered out of the room, its ample front and behind moshing in unison to the squeaky shuffle of sneakers.

What just happened? I thought as I lay there. *Where am I? Why do I feel like death? Maybe because I am dead? So, it's not so bad after all. But then why would I be feeling anything? Can this be heaven? Hell no. Surely people don't defecate in heaven? And if I was dead how could I think, and therefore how could I be?*

As you can tell, I was focused on humanity's most pressing metaphysical conundra. Ultimately though, it was not Cartesian logic that won me over to my continued existence. Rather, it was the very physical sensation of needing to scratch my unreachable testicles that verified I was not even in purgatory, but in a very terrestrial hospital, and that the lady I had just unwittingly harassed was a nurse. Which meant the dream I'd been having about a nun with a penchant for petroleum jelly was sadly just that, a dream. A dream that I decided to do my best to rejoin.

"Mr. Goodenough? Giles? Can you hear me? You are lucky to be alive."

I don't know whether several seconds, minutes, or hours

had passed, but the next thing I remember was a man leaning over me. Fortunately, the balloon of my revived arousal was punctured, as men just don't do it for me. The voice was very self-impressed. The tone of someone certain he knew everything. Must be a doctor, I deduced.

"His vitals are okay, but he seems to be unconscious still, nurse. I think he must have been hallucinating. It's to be expected as his brain comes out of the coma."

"I dunno," said a voice immediately identifiable as the nurse I had assaulted. "He was talkin'. He sure thinks he knows who he is. He was even correctin' how I said his name and all."

"What else did he say?"

"Nothin'. He was too busy squeezin' my boobs."

The doctor chuckled lasciviously. "Who can blame him? I can't wait to get my hands back on those puppies. How about a quickie in the bathroom?"

"Shush…stop it," the nurse protested. "At the end of the day, no one knows. Not even my best friends. That's real talk. Let's keep it our secret, Dr. McHorny."

I knew she was fighting a losing battle as the two outlines came together into a single geometrical unit, which then moved with stifled grunting and rustling out of my range of vision. Somewhat jealously, I forced myself to ignore the lustbirds and tried to work out two key things. Why was I alive, and why was I almost dead?

Egon. The PEACH.

I must have drifted off again because I reverted to the dream I'd been having before the nurse woke me. The nun was putting the latex gloves back on.

Should I be telling you all this? Probably not. My father

wouldn't approve—even now. *Tutum silentii premium*, as he always used to tell me; i.e., shut up.

But I promised Cherry that when I wrote this down, I'd tell the whole story. And as luck would have it, I don't have enough self-respect, despite my new outlook on life, to avoid the nitty-gritty. I suspect I'll get away with the truth, though at times you might find it hard to believe. As my friends tell me, the truth of my fortunate life is often less believable than a lie. There's a reason they call me Lucky Jill.

As my poor mother said through her machine as she died, *All is for the best.*

BILLIONAIRE POS

I GUESS THE best place to start this story is with the lead-up to my first day at POS Capital, about eight months before my hospital visit.

I had already been in New York for a decade, ever since my father found me a job at Merrill Lynch. Not that it was the real Merrill Lynch by that stage. It was Bank of America, though no one in the office could bring themselves to say so.

Prior to that, I'd been bumbling around in London for almost all of the previous decade (I like to round things to the decade—the legacy of a Classical education, perhaps). I spent a lot of time there trying not to find meaningful employment and succeeded almost to a fault. Not quite though, as I earned just enough to prove my father's point that Classics was the doorway to a City Career. I didn't bother explaining to him that accountancy was a career in the city as opposed to a City Career, and he didn't seem to care. As I had a small trust fund, no one was going to notice. And as I spent more time playing squash and partying at Annabel's than auditing financial statements, in some ways I did have a City *lifestyle* at the least, replete with Hooray Henries, Hefty Hetties, and Horny Housewives (no, I'm not a saint, as you should already have gleaned).

Truth be known, I was lucky to have a job at all, given that I'd almost been sent down from Oxford after a particularly rambunctious evening at The Piers Gaveston. Giles Toogood got the blame. Giles Goodenough miraculously escaped. He (I) was far from a genius. But not far enough to completely fail out. In fact, I'd squeaked a 2.1 after the gentleman sitting next to me in finals sailed to a First. As I said, I'm not a saint.

Well, there I was at the Ad Cod pub one night, trying to beat out the prior evening's hangover by preparing for the next morning's (a futile task as I have discovered many times before and since), when who should stride in but my father, with more than his usual air of pompous gravity.

"*O tempora, o mores*," he intoned—one of his most over-used aphorisms. And within a month, I was back in New York, my childhood home.

It turns out that Father had finally got to grips with what I was (not) doing in London and had decided that it was time I got a real City Career in New York City. So, in his inimitable way he had picked up the phone to an old friend and gotten me one. And I was not one to reject it. My father's monumental force of will was only rivaled by my monumental apathy. There wasn't even a skirmish, let alone a battle. No matter what I did, he'd still be disappointed in me. So why bother fighting?

Thus it was that I ended up in Equity Research at Merrill Lynch in New York. As I had a degree in Classics, and a background in auditing insolvent grocery stores and gyms in the UK, they decided to launch me as a technology analyst covering Internet and New Tech (i.e., uncategorizable bubble stocks) in the US. I didn't have a clue what I was doing. I fitted right in. In many cases the companies didn't have a clue what they were doing either, so it all made perfect sense.

In the land of the blind, the blind man may not be king, but he is absolutely free to hang around. And I hung around for so long that some people began to believe I actually had half an eye, and I became a "well-respected expert" on the street.

My theories were the worst kind of popular tripe, my methods sloppy, and my conclusions highly questionable, as someone once said. I was a regular on CNBC. And I equally regularly updated my price targets to a reasonable 20 percent above wherever any stock currently traded, or more, if necessary, so I could retain at all times the highest price target on the street (my target, incidentally, was highest on the street in *all* my stocks, unless they went down, when I would quickly, under the cover of a Friday evening, become the lowest on the street).

My entire upbringing had encouraged me to go with the flow, and I was rewarded for my flexible mediocrity and promoted to vice president (which is just two notches down from being relevant). I had traveled far.

And thus it was that I came to cover what you all must know by now has been one of the great "story stocks" of the century, Zyxview. Launched by Egon Crump a decade ago (yes, again), my career at Merrill perfectly mirrored its inexorable march "up and to the right," as they say in the business. I was one of its earliest promoters, largely because, by a stroke of luck, it launched the week I started, and no one more senior could be bothered to cover it.

Every time Egon announced a new aspiration, I was the first to upgrade the stock. Okay, I couldn't actually upgrade it as I already had a "Conviction Buy" rating from day one (as I did on all my stocks that were going up); but I came up with the brilliant insight that creating a new category called

"Certain Buy" was a grammatical way of creating more trading business. Once all the juice was squeezed from that move, I added it to my "Best of the Best" list. I even suggested creating a new list called "Bestest of the Best," but apparently Goldman had already trademarked that.

In any case, to get back to where I was going to begin, it was through my coverage of Zyxview that I came to the attention of Peter O. Silver, the eponymous leader of hedge fund POS Capital.

I recall it as if it were yesterday (it was only just over a year ago, but don't let that dampen your surprise). I had just goal-seeked my latest models to create 20 percent upside for all my stocks that were going up. And I was just setting my out-of-office reply to explain I would be out till the following Tuesday, and was getting ready to leave for the Hamptons (the early part of the season being the best). As on most (Wednes) days I was also nursing a sacrilegious hangover, as Cherry had thrown a party at our place the night before for her Instagram followers and friends.

Anyway, I digress. The point is that I might have missed the call if I hadn't thought it was my voicemail calling me to complain that my mailbox was full again. Without so much as looking, I picked up the handset and put it back down. It rang again almost instantaneously. I was furious with our IT department but picked up, and this time held it tentatively to my ear. Bizarrely there was a human voice on the other end. Do people even use the telephone anymore?

It turns out that Peter O. Silver does, for reasons that will become understandable.

"Giles Goodenough?"

"He's out at the moment. Can I take a message?"

"Ah good, I'm glad I got you. This is Peter Silver." He doesn't think of himself as a genius for nothing.

"Ah, Peter, yes." That name hit me as hard as the rum floater in Cyril's BBCs (before the Daughters of the American Revolution over at the Maidstone Club had it shut down). Everyone knew Peter Silver. The Big Swinging Dick of the moment. The kind of guy who would steal a dollar from your grandma to ratchet himself up a spot in the Forbes 400. Piece of Silver Silver they (rather unimaginatively) called him. Others came up with a slightly more predictable (and even less imaginative) moniker for his hedge fund: POS Capital.

"You start on Monday, Giles."

"Actually, I'm out till Tuesday," I replied. I can't remember if I was trying to joke. It was the kind of glib remark that I default to.

"Not good enough," he roared, and then broke into laughter at his witticism. "See you Monday, then."

"Excellent," I replied, using the word my British education mandated for such awkward moments.

And that was that.

POS CAPITAL

I SHOWED UP the following Tuesday. That was my first mistake but not my last. Though a jest in keeping with my cultivated diffidence, apparently it didn't sit well.

"I'm docking you a day's pay, and ten percent of your annual bonus, should you get one," said Peter bluntly. I acquiesced pathetically. Jesting had its limits.

"What am I being paid?" I asked nonchalantly.

"Half as much as you would have been," he growled. I found out later that month that it was twice as much as I had been paid at Merrill, so net-net the impertinence paid off, I guess.

The truth is I had left Bank of America (now that I had left, I soon began referring to it contemptuously as such) without so much as a goodbye. Fortunately, I was able to DocuSign the non-compete. Apparently, no one even knew I'd left. An eager beaver called Dipak Shrivastava took over my coverage and, armed with my circular models, immediately did the right thing and raised all the price targets from 20 percent to 30 percent above that week's prices. Many people were convinced he'd been at B of A for years. "Well done on your Zyxview call," he was constantly told, according to my friends who still worked there (okay, acquaintances). B of A even continued to pay my salary for the first six months of my time at POS. When they asked for it back, I refused, and thanks to a clerical error and strong quarterly earnings, they generously added a hefty leaving bonus and forgot about me.

Why did I leave? I'm not sure actually. Perhaps because I thought it was worth it in order to show up on Tuesday rather than Monday. Or perhaps it was because I'd always been intrigued by the "buy-side"—that is the people who actually "invest" in equities rather than simply trade them for a commission, or make recommendations on them (to generate the trades that result in the commissions).

I don't think it was just for the money. It was partly for the money undoubtedly. I wanted to impress Cherry and give her the lifestyle I thought she wanted to become accustomed to. My B of A salary only went so far, and advisors, promising better returns while raising fees, were gobbling up the turkey trust fund, it seemed. What a surprise. I also wanted to earn so much that even my cold, distant, and unimpressed father might think I was worthy of a nod of congratulation. More than a nod was, sadly, an impossible objective.

Partly though, as I look back at the last year, it was sheer star-fucking (I could have been more vulgar but just chose today's dinner-table terminology). I wanted to see what Peter's life was like. I wanted to smell the aura of Billionaire.

In today's society, you see, billionaire has become adjectival. CNBC doesn't dare bring anyone of even a modicum of self-important smugness onto their channel without attaching the qualification "billionaire" to them if at all possible (you don't even have to be one, just seem to be one). "Billionaire investor, billionaire entrepreneur, billionaire convict." All are equally seductive, equally alluring to their anchors and viewers. Once you are a billionaire, you are no longer a person; you are a category, a synecdoche for something that we apparently all want, something that gets our juices flowing and our endorphins humming, like "the crown" used to be in days of yore, I suppose. The fact that you are usually a lucky, entitled, unpleasant twat (English terminology) is far from relevant. Welcome to America.

I guess that ever since I had returned to the States, I had slowly been lulled into judging my success by the number of billionaires I was near to at any given moment (to this point none). To get as close to one as I would be just by walking into the palatial chambers of POS Capital must have subconsciously pulled my trigger. So there I was, day one, on the receiving end of an immediate pay cut, and as happy as a Roman pleb in the presence of Caesar.

Perhaps the more important question is why they hired me. It turns out that it was on a completely false pretext, which was the most I had going for me. I was informed by my trader later that week that someone had told Holton Wynn, Peter's COO, that someone had told them that they knew someone who knew I had "very good information" on Zyxview. Having covered the company for a decade, I was too embarrassed to tell them that I'd never even met Egon, let alone that I had no really good information (or much information at all). As I told you in some detail (perhaps too much), my entire *modus operandi* had been to simply have the highest price target on Wall Street. I copied and pasted most of the "analysis" from various industry reports. And as Zyxview's products were too secretive to be produced (yet), that was already probably more analysis than most.

So I grinned and nodded vacuously when Peter informed me that he was accumulating a large position in Zyxview. He hadn't asked me about any information at all, let alone of the "very good" kind, so I hoped he was just going to take it on my gesture that he was doing the right thing.

"Someone read your stuff and loved it. 'Brilliant,' someone

called it," he grumbled. "Clearly you know this company inside out. Right? I'm doing the right thing buying this, right?" The pause was more expectant than pregnant.

As the stock had gone up almost every month since inception, I felt it was relatively riskless to answer with a wink. "Yes, absolutely." I don't know why I winked. It may have just been a blink engendered by the over air-conditioned office. But as I was having a conversation parallel to his shoulder (he never appeared to take his gaze off the sixteen monitors in front of him during trading hours), he caught it out of the corner of his eye and interpreted it as a wink. Okay, it probably was a wink. Second mistake.

"Never, ever wink at me again," he barked.

"Okay, boss."

"And never, ever call me boss again," he barked again. Third mistake. I shut up.

"Make sure you know more about Zyxview than Zyxview knows. Go."

I went.

Shuffling across to the far corner of the third floor of the office, head down, I slumped into my new open cubicle—FYI, cubicles were reserved for irrelevant flunkies, with all the (self-) important people surrounding Peter in the center of the trading floor. The smell of Billionaire was strong, but not quite as sweet as it had been when I took my first steps out of the elevator.

It was dead silent in the office, despite at least two hundred people doing their best pretending to be working. It was also freezing. The AC was dialed down to sixty-five even though the temperature outside was clocking in at a toasty ninety-five. Peter was doing his bit for global warming. I later discovered, by the way, that his wife had adopted climate change as her *cause célèbre*, giving over $100M of "his" money to various organizations that spent 80 percent on wining and dining their donors, and 20 percent on giving poor people in the third world the chance to save the planet. But if Peter wanted it cold and quiet, Peter got it cold and quiet: after all, "My name's on the fucking door," as he liked to put it.

To be fair, Peter's fleece-clad army of hundreds was permitted the occasional whoop or high-five if something particularly exciting happened. And of course, the only thing that ever qualified as exciting was the instantaneous generation of obscene profits for Peter and, by the simple math of trickle-down economics, themselves. Hey, if it worked for America, it worked for POS. Scraps from the king's table were plentiful if gobbled up with sufficient debasement.

A quick word on the office, as it deserves a long one. Its scale and design were predictably Billionaire-monumental. In fact, to call it an office or a trading floor at all tends to bathos, comprising as it did the top three floors in one of the largest towers in midtown Manhattan (conveniently just a block away from Harry Winston, Caviar Russe, and a Starbucks). It was more like a trading arena, and it had been meticulously modified to Peter's exact specification.

The overriding architectural concept consisted of three tiered concentric pentagons, set in the middle of the square tower, all of their vertices touching the outer walls. On the base floor, this meant a pentagonal main space with offices of increasing depth in the four triangular areas between the room and the wall of the tower. The second floor felt more normal as you entered. Identical offices lined a square perimeter. From the offices led several rows of trading desks that converged in the center. What was unusual was that the center consisted of a pentagonal hollow, with four staircases leading down to the center of the floor below. The third floor felt like the second, except that its hollow was smaller, and it had no stairs leading down; instead, if you leaned over the rails (which I did whenever Peter was out of the office, i.e., rarely), you would see straight down the two flights to where the "magic happens," as Peter liked to say, without even a modicum of irony.

In some ways the space closely resembled an amphitheater, which is maybe why I'm dwelling on it. I wrote a brilliant paper on the geometry and purpose of amphitheaters at Oxford, largely because I had acquired, literally, access to someone else's even more brilliant paper on the geometry and purpose of amphitheaters. *Again*, I'm no saint.

In terms of the dramatic effects of an amphitheater, however, the contrasts couldn't have been more extreme. An amphitheater encourages the audience to feel comfortable, anonymous in their seating far above the central stage, turning the focus of hundreds upon the few actors who strut and fret their way through the action. POS's pentagonal tiers were constructed such that everyone away from the central "stage" on the bottom floor could see very little of what was going on around them.

From that central zone, however—especially the circular pod of desks at its nucleus—a lot could be made out, and it purposefully made everyone else feel on edge ("edge" being critical for the hedge fund industry, perhaps). On the bottom floor each row of trading desks converged at Peter's central pod. And on the upper floors, each row would have converged there if the pentagonal hollow had not severed them. As a result, all sounds seemed to converge mathematically in Peter's ears. All sights did too, not only because of the natural lines of vision, but also because in the very center of the office, dangling some thirty feet from the skylight like some lunar landing craft at an aerospace museum, was a sculpture made entirely out of mirrors.

Conceived at vast cost by one of the most important artists

of the day—who had predictably earned her accolades pickling animals and making surreal cityscapes out of excrement—this was Peter's masterpiece, the central jewel in his Billionaire's crown. I can't remember its exact name, but it was something like *Shards of Light III*, or an equivalent pomposity. What I do admit was ingenious in its formulation (as all the art critics on Peter's payroll had agreed), was that it was one of the few "important" pieces of modern art that also served a utilitarian function. I once read an obsequious article in *Bloomberg Magazine* that quipped, "It should be considered the Sydney Opera House of the Hedge Fund World, not just a work of art, but an architectural expression masquerading as a work of art, a work of great perspicacity, and, like its owner, a tribute not just to its city but to our entire concept of who we are." Peter was on the board of Bloomberg.

Its more tangible brilliance lay in its ability to give a well-trained person, sitting in just the right place underneath its inverse apex, a kaleidoscopic view of the entire office, as each mirror had been meticulously placed to offer a discrete view of every desk, sometimes using other mirrors, unobtrusively placed on the walls and ceilings, to produce the perfect reflection. Peter had been sitting right underneath it for almost two decades, flanked by four of his most trusted lieutenants, the least trusted of whom was the COO, Holton Wynn.

"Giles Goodenough, stop staring and start working," boomed Peter's voice across the public address system. Clearly my gormless face had reflected into his peripheral vision. I zipped up my fleece and tried to turn on my computer. I failed at even that simple task.

SNATCH 2 & 20

MY FIRST FEW weeks on the job went by without a hitch. I was only almost fired twice.

But it became apparent soon after that my "I'm just tying up loose ends on my model" line was wearing thin. That was unfortunate, as it had worked perfectly at B of A. Even issuing a price target 40 percent above the current price didn't seem to be cutting it. I raised it to 50 percent, but to no avail. I had no idea what else I could do. Peter started to ask me more insistently about my "conviction level" and whether I had done "the work" to back it up. He also started to ask me what dates on the calendar would be the most important ones for the stock. When I suggested the earnings release dates, he almost punched me.

That's when Holton stepped in. In that brief moment of daily euphoria when Peter's Maybach pulled out of the garage and could be seen barging its way imperiously through traffic toward his Connecticut castle, Holton Wynn found where I pretended to work.

"Come on, Giles, let's get a drink."

Three hours later and three martinis in, I'd learned more about POS than in the previous month.

"So, you are saying that I actually need to get to know Egon," I choked.

"That's pretty much how it works."

"And then get information from him about Zyxview's products, financials, launch dates, and upcoming announcements, and communicate those to Peter in code."

"I never said that."

"What did you say?"

"I said that you need to get to know Egon in order to know the company better than anyone, including all the upcoming catalysts for the stock, which will enable us to be ahead of everyone else trying to do the same thing. It's how Peter makes money."

"But isn't that what I said?"

"No. What you said would be insider trading."

"How would I know all the catalysts if I don't ask him those questions?"

"I don't know. That's for you to work out." I could have sworn he winked, but perhaps it was a blink.

Whatever the nuances that were for the moment escaping me, it was pretty clear that I was expected to cheat from day one. My objection was not purely on moral and legal grounds (though no saint, I draw a line at felonies). It also implied that I was going to have to hustle and work. That was an entirely new concept for me, and I was pretty upset.

"Did you ever cover a company for Peter?" I asked hopefully, trying to get the inside scoop on getting the inside scoop.

"Nah. I would never do that. I love my family too much."

"So how did you get to be COO?"

"I played lacrosse at Virginia."

I assumed he'd misheard. The dimly lit room was packed full of other men, sipping the same cocktails at other similar tables, no doubt all having similar hushed conversations. It wasn't even late enough for the hookers at the bar to be getting much attention.

"No, I asked how you got to be COO," I whispered more loudly.

"Yes, I played lacrosse at Virginia." Holton smiled. "You don't get it, do you?"

"Nope."

"Okay, so here is how the industry basically works. You've got the head guy, who's usually a sociopathic, autistic narcissist with a massive chip on his shoulder. He is determined to make more money than the next guy at all costs, so that others can find out he has more money than the next guy. But they can't do that without funds, which they have to raise from asset allocators."

"Okay..." I probed.

"The asset allocators usually come from the Midwest, or Texas, or somewhere. Pension fund money or the like. Dumb as shit. They aren't used to dealing with New York types. So, the New York types hire a jock to raise the money. Jocks are universally looked up to by asset allocators as they are the guys at high school who nailed all the cheerleaders the asset allocators had wet dreams over."

"Did you nail a lot of cheerleaders?"

"Hundreds—sometimes in pyramids. I tell the asset allocators about my days at Virginia, winning the NCAA, and the frat parties where the cheerleaders dressed like schoolgirls. They allocate hundreds of millions of dollars almost immediately. Nothing turns the spigots on like mental images of naked schoolgirls. Of legal age, of course." Did he wink again?

"Don't they want to meet Peter and study his track record?"

"Are you fucking kidding me? They don't give a shit about

that. Occasionally, you get one of the junior guys grazing around the office like a sheep, peeing himself in case he offends someone and fucks up the allocation. In any case, every track record looks good if you start and end it at the right point, exclude bad years, and compare it to a favorable index. Every hedge fund sucks over a long enough time frame when measured against the risk."

"Really?"

"Yup. Even when you know more than anyone else. That's how bad hedge funds are. It's the least best-kept secret on Wall Street. From time to time, I also get Peter to refuse someone's money if they ask too many questions. You've got to make it feel like a club that they are privileged to get into."

"Why?"

"So they don't ask too many questions, idiot. Peter doesn't want anyone sniffing around and actually getting a real idea of what he's doing. Bad for business."

"But what if he then loses them money, and they didn't even do proper diligence."

"They couldn't care less. Here's why. He never actually loses them money. He can't. At least that's what he tells me. The worst he can do is underperform the correct benchmark over time. But no one is looking at the correct benchmark, so it is irrelevant anyway."

I was going to ask a follow-up but hesitated.

"More importantly though," he went on, "as long as all the other asset allocators have invested, then even if they lose everything, they can say that everyone lost everything, and no one saw it coming. That is why they invest in swarms. Strength in numbers."

"I see," I said blankly. It's not that I had any moral qualms about it really. If they were foolish enough to invest when they shouldn't have, then that was capitalism at its best, right? Caveat emptor, and all that.

"Remember as well that the asset allocators are collecting a nice fat fee managing money for pension funds and the dumb kids of successful businessmen. So as long as they don't rock the boat, they get to have the biggest house in Des Moines and send their kids to the only private school in town, where they can also unsuccessfully try to bang the cheerleaders before becoming asset allocators. And so it goes on."

"All is for the best," I proffered.

"I don't know about that." Holton laughed. "All is for Peter, more like."

"The wheels of capitalism?" I suggested irrelevantly.

"Exactly," chimed in Holton unexpectedly, his eyes now starting to swim like a preteen at a Justin Bieber concert. "Everyone knows their place in this great financial economy. The guys at the bottom sweat, the guys in the middle work, and the few guys at the top charge two percent on everyone's assets, and twenty percent on their profits for good measure. Two and twenty. Every single year. If the stock market goes south, their buddies from business school at the Federal Reserve cut interest rates or print money to jack prices back up. And they have to. If they don't, the whole leaning tower will come crashing to earth with everyone trapped inside. It's jerry-rigged extortion, and all the one-percenters are in on the game. It's a brilliant con to be honest.

"And it's not just hedge funds," he continued. I couldn't tell now if he was elated or furious, or somewhere in between. He was certainly getting agitated. "Look at private equity. Those fricking assholes might be the worst of the lot. They use cheap money the Fed prints to buy companies with debt, increase prices to consumers, fire half of the workforce, underinvest in the long-term success of the business, pay themselves out huge dividends, and then sell the shell of what's left to the next private equity fund, or one of their buddies from Andover who's CEO somewhere. He writes it down as worthless in a few years when no one notices, and the game moves on. They can't even outperform the goddamn stock market. But the asset allocators are still all over them: they want to be them, you see. It's pathetic."

"But remunerative."

"Exactly," he said, working himself up to a climax. "So the PE boys pocket their billions, and even their minions get fat from the kings' scraps. It's great work if you can get it. Meanwhile the workers they've so enthusiastically thrown on the streets are still paying thirty percent plus federal tax that year on their marginal income, while the PE crooks have stitched up the tax code so they only pay twenty percent federal tax on their billions in profits. Then, if some single mother, struggling to raise a family in some cockroach-infested apartment in the Bronx, so much as dares suggest they pay more in tax, they launch an all-out multimillion-dollar PR blitz explaining to the guy in the street what geniuses they really are, how the entire American economy relies on them—'creative destruction' or some horseshit—and how they are all ready to pay more in tax anyway even if they shouldn't have to."

"That's BS," I chimed in, now that his antipathy was clear.

"Of course it's BS, Giles. You see, at the same time they just double their expenditure to the lobbyists and politicians to stop higher taxes on their profits. And they double their tax-deductible private jet hours flying around the world to conferences explaining to each other and the politicians in their pockets how great the system is for everyone, not just them. The fawning media—also owned incidentally by their other buddies—parrots their narrative, leaving good old Joe Shmoe focusing on the NFL season, if he can afford the TV package. No wonder millennials are all socialists."

"My wife's a millennial," I replied, "and she's not a socialist. You might be though."

"I'm one hundred percent not a socialist," he said as defensively as if I'd called his mother a whore. "Remember, I have to keep up with the others. We'd all be happier if the entire system collapsed, but until it does, I'm the biggest capitalist of the lot, brother. I was kind of counting on the millennials to bring it all down though. What's wrong with your wife?"

"She makes far too much on Instagram to be a socialist," I explained, "selling makeup to other millennials and creepy old guys who really just want to fuck her."

"Awesome. About the only way to make money as an insolvent millennial is by selling stuff to other insolvent millennials, or your body to old rich dudes—either virtually or literally. And the best part is that someone has convinced young chicks that selling their bodies on some sugar daddy website is actually empowering. I've got to be honest, dude. The whole thing is so brilliant it would be sad to see it go. You can't make this stuff up."

"Another drink for you guys?" suggested our waitress (sorry, I mean server), who had frisked her way across the room and sidled up to us flirtatiously, hoping no doubt to trade her short dress and long legs for a large tip. I hoped she hadn't heard the end of our conversation.

"No, we are fine. We'll get the check please, darling," said Holton while ogling her perky tits. I suspected he was a regular on the sugar daddy websites he seemed to know so much about.

"Sure thing," she replied with the needless enthusiasm of the young and dumb, and headed off to her terminal.

"Come on, Giles. Let's go see some titties without clothing ruining them." Holton grinned while keeping his eyes fixed on her tight posterior.

"A strip club?"

"You got it."

"No, I can't," I replied sheepishly.

"Why the hell not?"

"My wife will find out."

"No she won't. What's the matter with you? Balls already removed? English education? You're not gay, are you? How would she possibly find out?"

"Because she's a stripper," I confessed.

"SWEET! I love it. You dirty dog. Okay, we'll call it a night. No questions asked."

"Actually, I do have one more question," I added as we stumbled out into the fading light. "Who exactly recommended me for this job? I wanted to say thanks."

"No idea. I think Peter discovered you all on his own."

"But my trader told me that it was your recommendation."

"Nope. Never heard of you before Peter put your résumé on my desk and told me to hire you. Take it easy, pal. And remember. All you need to do…"

"…is know more about Zyxview than anyone else," I concluded.

"You are learning fast."

And with that Holton jumped into the back of his limo and headed off, to a strip club, no doubt.

CHERRY

TO BE FAIR on her, her name is Cheryl. Cherry is her stage name.

She grew up on a farm in Iowa and soon after went into "the business"—that is "dancing" (i.e., stripping with a few soft porn titles to her credit). I know that sounds clichéd. But I can only hide behind the truth.

Unsurprisingly, I met her at a "gentleman's club" (has there ever been a more blatant misnomer?) about five years earlier, and was immediately smitten for reasons both obvious and recondite. The obvious ones were blonde hair, blue eyes, 36DD-24-36 (and before you call me a pig, remember I am just an ape, and just like every man you know), and lips that gave her the nickname Cherry. The more abstruse reasons were the way she smiled with her eyes, the way her nose turned up like my mother's, and the way she clearly had no interests in the world beyond herself, her followers, and, bizarrely, Ovaltine.

I'm not quite sure why she liked me. Nor was she, I think (I don't *know* as she doesn't really analyze). Perhaps I seemed like a follower, ethically and digitally. Or perhaps because I, also, like Ovaltine. Perhaps she sensed a lost soul, or just one that wanted an easy life. Perhaps she liked my slight English

accent. Or perhaps she liked my diffidence, carefully cultivated at St. Paul's and Oxford.

Or perhaps she just thought I was rich (by her standards).
She certainly seemed to love me a lot more when she found
out that I was an investment banker and had supplemental
income from a small trust fund established by my paternal
grandfather, who pioneered a technique for force-feeding turkeys to achieve the perfect weight in time for Thanksgiving.

I'm not saying that I don't have looks. When I glance in
the mirror, I see a fairly standard all-American face with just
a dash of the exotic. My BMI clocks in at a solid twenty-
eight. Some of it is even muscle. And I'm not saying I don't
appear to have pedigree. My father, after all, claims to trace his
lineage from the Dukes of Escumesthorpe (at least my admis-
sion to the Bullingdon and his perennial haughtiness were on
that basis). The fact that Escumesthorpe is the modern-day
Scunthorpe, a miserable town of gray clouds and grayer build-
ings in the industrial north of England, was never deduced.
Nor, fortunately, did anyone bother to corroborate its historical accuracy.

But I certainly don't look like the men she was used to
cavorting with on the set of *My Princess's Diaries I*. Or *II, III,*
or *IV* for that matter. I have watched them all, beginning to
end. The acting is probably the best part. Or maybe the pecs.

I was certainly no stallion. But I seemed to please her
from our first date, which began as soon as her shift ended on
that snowy January evening. We married six months later. My
father's prejudice for her Germanic pedigree (Goodenough
was an upgrade from Schilthorn) quickly overcame his prejudice for her lowly upbringing and nonexistent education. He
even walked her down the aisle (her father having recently
been mauled to death by a rabid John Deere).

The wedding itself was a true spectacle, less because of the grandeur of its setting (her mother spent half of her late husband's life insurance on it, and it still was little more than a barn dance), and more due to the incongruous apposition of drunk English toffs and a motley assortment of New York "dancers" and Iowan farmers. I certainly think I can lay claim to having had the only wedding (in Iowa) that ended up with all of the groomsmen and all of the bridesmaids "getting lucky" in the same room at the same time, or so I am told, frequently. I had already passed out face down in Cherry's ample bosom by that stage of the morning.

Our married life was bliss. She did what she wanted (accumulate followers and work out, mostly), and I did what I wanted. And we met up occasionally to practice procreation. We'd also been mature enough, or so we judged, to deal with extramarital lust. As an ex-stripper and farmgirl who had seen animal urges in action, she felt it would be inviting disaster to jeopardize our marriage over an occasional slipup, at least at this early stage when we were childless and young. I suggested we limit what atavistic society calls infidelities to oral sex. She liberally advocated for one-night stands. We settled somewhere in the middle. Neither of us was quite sure where, but we felt we'd be able to judge case by case. Lack of emotional involvement with the other party was obviously critical. So far the system had worked perfectly.

❧

When I got home after drinks with Holton that evening, I found Cherry taking selfies in one of the many mirrors in our apartment. No surprise there. What was a little surprising though was that she was wearing clothes. Clearly these photos were for public consumption.

"Hi, honey."

"Hi, sweetie."

"Where've you been? Scooping the loop?"

"I guess so," I replied. "If that includes having drinks with the COO of POS."

"Wowsers, aren't you important now."

"I have always been important," I returned with a smile. "How about you? What've you been up to?"

"Just messin' around. What do you think of the new shade?" she asked, puckering her lips into a perfect sphere. "I'm launching next week."

"Gorgeous," I enthused, despite the fact that it looked the same as the previous new shade.

The banalities continued for a couple of minutes till we ran out of banalities. Later that evening, as I disengaged from her with a sigh, she could tell something was wrong.

"Wasn't that good for you, prince? Do we need to try again?"

"No, it was great. I'm just a little stressed out at work."

"Oh no, honey, what's wrong?"

"Well, for a start they are actually asking me to do something."

"Hell no, I'm going to go right over there and teach them a lesson," she jested, with a spank to my behind. "Naughty boys."

"I know." I grinned, mostly in satisfaction that she was beginning to respond appropriately to irony, like a dog that finally pees in the right spot. "Apparently, I've got to know more about this damned company than anyone else, including the CEO. How exactly am I supposed to do that?"

"Get to know the CEO?" she offered, after a momentary pause to formulate this invaluable insight.

"I guess so. I'll just have to trust my luck."

"What does your father always say, carpet deem?"

"*Carpe diem*, I think you'll find. *Vitae summa brevis spem nos vetat incohare longam.*" Now I was just taunting her.

"Oh, you are so funny." And with that she fell into a deep sleep. And I into a deeper funk.

I hadn't told Cherry the full story, of course, specifically Holton's not-so-subtle indication that what Peter wanted was specific, material, non-public information. Not that she would have understood what that was, or my attempts to explain it. But she would have understood what up to twenty years in the federal penitentiary meant. And that's what I was looking at if I got caught doing what, apparently, everyone else at POS did. It was fraud, plain and simple, and it was wrong. And I wanted no part of it. My laissez-faire attitude did have its limits, I discovered, when prison rape was a possible consequence.

But that seemed to leave me with only one option, to resign a few weeks after starting, which would be fodder to my father's conviction that I was a failure, and imply that I cared enough to take the moral high ground, which could be devastating to my marriage, which depended, I believed, on money and a cynical nonchalance. Maintaining the latter would be easier than finding a similarly lucrative job, or any job at all.

I had the feeling that Peter wouldn't be writing me a stellar reference, and the unwritten rule at the banks was that if you left for the "buy-side," you were never coming back. My trust fund would only keep us housed, clothed, and fed, and not much more, in New York City. So calling it quits would be devastating. I felt like a chump for having thought that I could transfer my laziness to POS and simply pick up a fortune for doing the same non-work. But then isn't that "all is for the best" attitude the root of who I am? God knows.

By about 3 a.m. I had come up with the best solution I could think of. It wasn't very good. But then squaring a circle isn't easy. I would try to get to know Egon. That in itself would likely prove impossible, so I could resign. If by some miracle I found myself alone with Egon, I would make it clear that he should only discuss with me what he thought was non-material. The likely outcome of that would be that Peter would fire me. But I spied a glimmer of hope that somehow I could convince Peter that I had inside information, when in fact I didn't, while at the same time having enough information to continue to recommend Zyxview without fearing Peter's wrath. If you're a little confused as to how I intended to stay balanced on this ethical high wire, all I can say is you are probably less confused than I was. But then that shouldn't surprise you, as I'm always pretty confused when confronted with complexity.

Fortunately, there was nothing complex about Cherry's naked body. I knew exactly how to nuzzle her breasts, and fell asleep at last.

SAUSAGE-FEST

THE FOG WAS heavy as I landed in SFO. Which had meant the usual delays and usual excuses, all capped by a cheery "We hope you had a nice flight and thank you for *choosing* Delta." No, I did not, either way. And no mention of the half hour of diving and shearing we had experienced over Iowa. The irony was not lost on me, of course. The metaphysical one was more mordant than the geographic one.

I had journeyed to San Francisco to get to know Egon, somehow. And I had chosen the most obvious route: the Merrill Lynch Tech Conference. I was almost bound to fail, as he wasn't even going to be there. But it beat sitting in New York. And I fantasized that the CFO, who *was* scheduled to speak, might be convinced to make an introduction. I wasn't delusional enough to hold out much hope, and I was ready to resign the day I returned.

If you haven't been to one of these conferences (I hadn't), let me enlighten you. First, on why I'd never been to one. You see, there are two things you need to know about me that may have not yet become fully apparent. I am terrified of death (my mother died when I was six, so I blame it on that), and I am terrifically lazy (partly inherited, partly cultivated—effort still being seen as very *infra dig* in British high society). So I never wanted to fly anywhere, and I never wanted to waste time working, when everything seemed to be going just swimmingly without so much as getting in a taxi. People at Merrill misconstrued it as meaning I was so well connected that I didn't need to meet other investors, let alone management teams. And I wisely did nothing to disabuse them of that false supposition. Why jinx my serendipity? The worst thing that could happen would be for me to lose conviction in any company whose stock was going up, or worse still, gain conviction in a company whose stock was going down. The goal-seek function in Excel had been invented for that purpose. Who was I to outthink Bill Gates? They say price is all that matters, and I made that my mantra.

As it happened, it took me less than a day to realize my prior lackadaisical approach had been true edge.

Picture this. Ballrooms packed full of twenty- and thirty-something b-school grads furiously scribbling down every word a company management team says, while exchanging furtive glances and knowing nods. A productive sausage-fest? Not even. Because of Reg FD (passed in 2000 to stop selective disclosure of information by companies at events just like this) everything the management had ever said was available on their website. Hell, even their presentation that day was available on their website. And even if it hadn't been available already, there was no point noting what they were saying as everyone else was noting it. And as everyone else represented about 95 percent of all investment funds, that meant that no one would know anything that every other buyer and seller didn't already know. So what was the point?

A cynic might say there wasn't one. Which is what I say. But I discovered—when I asked my friend Tom in the coffee break between these charades—that there were some in the industry (another glaring misnomer, as it connoted hard work) who apparently claimed that they could tell from management "tone" how things were really going. When I asked Tom if he could, he admitted he couldn't. When I asked him if he knew of any who could, he slapped me on the back and headed to get a front row seat at the next presentation.

The "one-on-one" meetings were no better. Apparently, these were the only reason most people bothered coming in the first place, at least the non-clairvoyants from the bigger funds. Sequestered in hotel bedrooms above the main event space like cheap hookers, management teams would hunker down with a few "select investors" to give them the real scoop. In another prime example of the trickle-up principles of the financial industry, only those investors who did big business with the bank would be invited to participate. As POS was the biggest gorilla in the zoo, I got invited to all of them. I went to one.

&

I arrived on time to Dynapro's session in room 703. I had no idea what Dynapro did. You see, I'd only been covering it for three years, and as it was 50 percent below its all-time high, I had a "Certain Sell" on it, 20 percent below the current price. What more does one need to know, I wondered?

It seems the first thing to know is never to turn up on time. By the time I arrived, the meeting had already been going on ten minutes, I was told. I needn't have worried. They were still just running through the presentation they had just given, in the same monotone. I mumbled some confused apologies and took a seat on the radiator. An uptight lady clearly from IR frowned and wrote something down. I thought it would be churlish to point out that I was on time, and so hung my head like a puppy that has defecated on a Persian rug for the second time in a morning. I glanced up again to see Tom sitting on the other radiator, looking equally miserable.

It turned out these meetings ended up being a little more useful on the surface, given that management took questions after wrapping up the presentation. However, the questions were really just attacks, which the management team had no inclination to indulge.

"How's the quarter looking?" asked a fat and sweaty twenty-something with an agitated demeanor. He looked as if the most exercise he'd enjoyed in the last year was with his mandible.

"We don't give updates on the quarter," sighed the CFO disparagingly, "...as you know, Jacob."

"How's business this quarter?" asked a bald veteran. I wasn't sure if he hadn't heard the previous reply, but it was irrelevant; no sooner had he spoken than the rest of the pack joined the fray.

"I heard from your customers that you're losing share."

"Your suppliers say you are extending payments."

"Your share price is in the tank, guys, and we've just about had enough of it."

"No one believes anything you say anymore."

The stock was 50 percent off its all-time highs, after all.

It appeared that these were less question-and-answer sessions than answer-and-berate sessions, with various insipid minions clunking steel Rolexes on the table while insulting the management team and telling them why things were going so badly (having already been told the opposite). If anyone was there to check out "tone," they must have left disappointed, as the management's only commentary involved them meekly referring to their 10-Q (i.e. quarterly report filed with the SEC). I also mused that even if management had broken the law and told them everything, it would have done them little good; everyone else in the room, or in one of the next ten sessions they were holding, would immediately know as much as everyone else. But perhaps the most bizarre part of the whole thing was that when the IR lady called an end to this Kabuki dance, all the investors jumped up and eagerly shook hands with the management team as if they were best friends.

"See you later, Ray." Jacob chortled with a born-again bonhomie.

෨

"Well, that seemed entirely worthless," I suggested to Tom as we retreated down the corridor toward the elevator.

"Are you kidding me?" he replied. "Management tone definitely changed from the last time I saw them."

"Really? How?"

"They seem a lot more upbeat."

"Are you sure?"

"Actually, I'm not so sure now you say it. Perhaps they were more downbeat. It definitely changed though."

"Interesting," I offered sportingly.

Poor Tom. I couldn't help but notice how much older he now seemed since he'd left Merrill Lynch in New York for the sunshine and healthy living of Silicon Valley a few years earlier. I'd been told at the time he'd made a huge mistake, and I now sensed that he knew it. You see, he'd left equity "research" to take a job at Fin Capital, a little known hedge fund in Palo Alto. Very low Billionaire points, as the head of the firm, Bryan Fisk, was only worth a couple of hundred. He never got on CNBC.

What made matters worse was that rumor had it they made the mistake of actually hedging their positions and remaining "market-neutral." As I had it explained to me, that meant when the market went up, they went up a little if they got everything right, and if the market went down, they likely just went sideways. It seemed to me that this was what hedge funds were supposed to do (from the little I knew), but I was wiser than to question the commentary.

What people were really trying to say, I surmised, was that the fastest way to get ahead was to go with the flow. And as that has always been the *sine qua non* of my approach to everything in life, I wasn't one to dispute it. Why bother hedging when everything goes up and to the right courtesy of the Federal Reserve and a broken economy (counterintuitively)? Their commitment to doing the right thing for their investors was laudable, perhaps, but very foolish, certainly. Two percent of not a lot of assets, and 20 percent of not a lot of profits, seemed like a foolish errand when the allocators were willing to open the spigots for a strategy that went up in line with the market as long as you pretended you were hedged. And seriously, who was ever going to check when they were too busy salivating at another story of the lacrosse team and its toga parties? Just snatch the two and twenty, and run for Palm Beach

If the market crashed, Fin Capital would look smart. But that was never going to happen, and moreover, if it did, no one could ever have seen it coming, right? So, far better to go with the flow, earn a ton of un-refundable cash, and close the fund if the market crashed, opening up again as a new fund at the start of the next cycle along with everyone else. Because everyone would know at that stage that the market would never crash again, and the manager who had lost them everything now had more "invaluable experience," which could justify even higher fees. Hey, some wily veterans like Peter now charged three and thirty. It seemed bizarre to me on reflection that he even bothered with inside information. But then I don't understand complex people any more than general complexity.

"What are you up to, Tom? Fancy a drink somewhere? I'd love to catch up."

"No way, man, sorry, I can't," replied Tom as the elevator returned to the main floor. "I have a ton more presentations and one-on-ones, and then it's the big Zyxview thing at three."

"What big Zyxview thing? I thought the CFO was coming in tomorrow."

"What, didn't you hear? Last minute. Egon himself is coming in for the first time ever. He's going to do a 'fireside chat.' It's the first time he's ever deigned to come to one of these events. Everyone is wondering what's up. Perhaps it's because after he beat up his girlfriend, the stock has had its first correction in years the last couple of weeks."

That much I knew, as it had coincided with my first few weeks at POS, of course. I'd responded by telling Peter that it was a great buying opportunity: there was now 60 percent upside to my target price. Always double down, right? And there was no way he could have expected me to know about Egon's personal life, right?

I let Tom go and mused on fate, while taking a restorative break in the over-marbled restroom. It was bad news that Egon had decided to come perhaps, but surely this was my one chance to get to know him better. I had it all planned out. I was going to arrive five minutes early. And with that I headed off to the hotel gym to check out the "tone" of my biceps (deteriorating).

THE COLOSSEUM

BY THE TIME I arrived ten minutes early to the 3 p.m. event, I was already half an hour late, apparently, and was ushered into a side room to watch the chat on a TV with fifty other disgruntled investors (including Tom). I'd blown my chance of getting close to Egon before I'd even had a chance to blow it. From where I was, I would have been better streaming the event from the office. Less stale odor.

The ballroom itself must have been packed to the gunnels, as even the murmurs could be heard through the walls separating the two rooms. As the TV screen came to life, two deep leather armchairs came into focus, a raging fire in between them. It looked like one of those free channels you can download on YouTube for Christmas to create a warm and cozy environment if you can't afford a fireplace of your own. Not that anyone at that conference had that problem. I think the principle was to lull the interviewee into a false sense of security so they would feel comfortable opening up more fully. Or at least that was the ludicrous precept.

Suddenly, the floor started to vibrate. The anticipation was reaching fever pitch next door, like the Colosseum at the arrival of a fresh batch of Christians. Whoops and yells came flooding through the wall. Caesar was clearly making an entrance. *Panem et circenses*, the zeitgeist of the current American social, economic, and political system. Who said Classics was irrelevant?

On the screen ran into view a creature guaranteed to excite the visceral instincts of the investing masses. I say creature because this humanoid was clad in animal skins. To be precise, black leather pants, brown leather flip-fops, and a luxuriant fur vest that wouldn't have looked out of place on one of Cherry's friends at Flashdancers. Mirrored sports shades were the only other accoutrement, unless you count the over-gelled spikes that counted for hair. Perhaps Egon had been told this was a "three pieces of clothing" party. In fact, he soon revealed he had just come from the office.

"How have you achieved so much in so little time?" asked Barry Smith, head of B of A (Merrill) Equity Research, like some boy introduced to the ghost of Babe Ruth. I winced at the softball. Everyone around me scribbled down the question.

"I don't want to answer that, Barry," said Egon seriously. The answer silenced the rooms. "I'm not here to talk about me. I'm here to talk about Zyxview. You see, Zyxview is more than just about me. It is about humanity, its future, our kids, and our planet." Roars of approval and waves of applause. Egon raised his hands imperiously. Silence returned instantaneously.

"Zyxview is up a thousand percent since we IPO'd ten years ago. But that is nothing compared to what it is going to be. You see, we've solved many of the most important issues facing the world in the next hundred years. We've had many skeptics— you know who you are, and I know where you live—but we've proved them wrong! You guys at Merrill have nailed it since day one, so props for that. You guys are fucking smart."

I smiled modestly and looked around expectantly. I needn't have bothered. No one had a clue who I was.

"Yeah, Egon," oozed Barry. "I think some people just don't get it. They point to the fact that you haven't launched any products and don't have any revenue, have burned through two billion in cash, have done multiple financing rounds, and so on."

Hushed silence. You could have heard a toga drop.

"Exactly," replied Egon with a sudden unironic fervor. "What I have built is an R&D team of historical importance. Imagine taking Leonardo, Edison, Marconi, Einstein, and me, and putting them in a room and saying, 'Solve the greatest problems confronting mankind in the twenty-first century, and do it in a way that rolls back the tide of climate change at the same time.' That is what we have done. Would you doubt that the solutions they came up with would change the world forever? Let me answer that for you, bozo. Never. Never. Never."

With that Egon jumped up and dabbed for the audience. It was his latest signature move, I was later told. One he claimed to have invented (despite all evidence to the contrary). The crowd went wild. At the bottom of the shot, the front rows were all dabbing in unison. And as everyone, except Tom, me, and a guy in wheelchair facing the wall, were dabbing in the side room, I had no doubt that the ballroom looked like a weird outtake from *The Triumph of the Will*. The guy in the wheelchair, to be fair on him, was trying. He just couldn't get his arms over his head.

"Hell yeah…" Egon continued. "Fuck yeah."

It took several minutes for Barry to regain control, both of himself and the audience.

"Egon, that's brilliant, that's awesome." More applause. "Now let's take a couple of questions that we've had WhatsApp'ed to us from the audience." This was clearly a lie, as no one in the Merrill Tech Team knew how to use

WhatsApp. But it sounded woke, so he went with it, before shamelessly taking a piece of paper out of his pocket.

"Sure, fire away," said Egon, sinking deep into the chair.

"When might we see revenue from one of your products?"

"When you see it."

"What exactly are the biggest problems facing humanity that Zyxview is aiming to solve?"

"The biggest ones. Next."

"How much more cash will you need till breakeven?"

"As much as I need. Next."

"What percentage of your net worth is invested in Zyxview?"

"All of it, except what I need to lead a fairly humble life. Next."

"How would you like to be remembered?"

"As the first man who lived forever. Hint. Next."

I could go on, but you get the idea. I decided to skim-read the *Wall Street Journal*. Within seconds, the entire side room was glaring at me, so I put it down.

"What a disaster," I said to Tom as we squeezed through the door half an hour later. "He failed to answer anything."

"He's a genius," replied Tom. "The stock's up thirty percent in the aftermarket."

"What? After that bullshit? Who the hell is buying in the aftermarket?" I mused aloud.

"We are covering our short," replied Tom stoically.

"Sorry," I said unconvincingly. Tom slumped off toward the over-marbled restrooms. I prayed that he'd live to see tomorrow.

⌇

I hung around in the lobby hoping to see Egon as he came out and introduce myself. He went out a back door, apparently.

I was distraught, despite receiving a call from Peter praising my analysis on the back of the aftermarket move. "How much more do you think it's got in it?" he inquired greedily.

"Well, I've clearly got some work to do on my model, but preliminary estimates would suggest there is at least another fifty percent upside based on what he said, and that's just in the short term."

"Excellent," said Peter. "Keep this up. And let me know anything else you learn from him when you chat to him later. Only public information, of course." I could almost see the smirk across the airwaves.

"Absolutely," I semi-lied. I would do, if I met him. I just wasn't going to meet him.

I sat down in an armchair as the hotel emptied. I had no idea what to do, or why I was even there. In such moments I relied on Cherry for moral support.

"Hi, honey."

"Oh hi, sweetie."

"What's up?"

"Knee high by the fourth here."

"What are you doing?"

"Just working on my glutes with DeShaun," she sighed. DeShaun was one of her bevvy of strapping personal trainers. Her glutes you can imagine. "He is such an angel. He's got such a soft way with him, despite being rock hard and as big as one of Dad's milkers."

"Thanks for the detail," I offered miserably.

"Oh sorry, honey. What's the matter?"

"I totally failed to meet with Egon even though he showed up at one of these things for the first time. It's impossible to get close to him. He's surrounded by adoring fans."

"Shucks," she sighed, distractedly, I thought. "By the way,

did you know that the best way to loosen your glutes is by a deep stretch of the abductors? It feels incredible."

"No I didn't, honey. I prefer to do the splits," I said bitterly.

"You're so funny, byeeee. Oh, by the way, if you're stressed go down to the Gold Club. They couldn't be sweeter there. If you mention my name, they'll give you free dances. If Jamie's there she might even give you a BJ if you say you're my husband."

As I've said, my wife was as liberal in our marriage as she was in her politics. It wasn't that she was a slut. It's just that in "the business," a blowjob is basically a handshake. I know, it's hard to understand if you come from the real world, if there is such a place.

"Well, that's something, I guess. Thanks for the tip," I said as nonchalantly as my frustrated anxiety allowed.

"That's what she'll say, honey." She laughed. Her sense of innuendo was primitive. "Just remember what your mother used to say; all is for the best." She gasped at something and hung up abruptly. Or perhaps she moaned. She sounded happy, anyway. Perhaps she was surfing Instagram while talking to me.

The Gold Club was the last place on earth I wanted to go at that moment, which was saying a lot, as I'm not immune to the charms of women (as you've already gleaned) and the benefits of an open-ish marriage. I sat blankly and self-pitied. As I saw it I'd given it my best, which was more than I'd ever done before. So I could be proud of that, though no one else would be. And I'd resign with Peter already up nicely on his Zyxview position. At least that was something. Perhaps I could go back into accounting?

"Hey, Giles…bud." A jockish voice woke me from my defeatist torpor. It was Barry Smith. I had no idea he knew who I was. He'd never even acknowledged me at Merrill (no doubt because I was his star analyst). I assumed I'd gained the Billionaire BO from joining POS, and that he now deemed me worthy of attention. I assumed wrong.

"Great job on Zyxview. That guy is sick good. This is the next Microsoft, Apple, and Amazon combined. As you always say. Good job raising the price target to thirty percent above the street. Twenty percent was never enough. You're our top guy."

Dipak Shrivastava's hard work had clearly gone unnoticed.

"I assume you're coming to dinner, as usual," he continued.

I'd never been to a work dinner with him (or anyone for that matter). I didn't know whether his delusions were calculated or medical. But compared to a BJ at the Gold Club, a night out with Barry seemed positively electrifying. That tells you how low I'd gotten.

"Sure, bro, where are you going and who's coming?" I was trying to speak his language. Perhaps Tom might not be hanging from the ceiling of the over-marbled restroom and would be there, I contemplated optimistically. Misery loves company, etc.

"Ha! That's funny. You Brits."

"I'm American."

"Nice. I'll see you at eight at Tadich. I'll put you next to him. I need your thoughts."

"Next to whom?" I offered properly.

"Egon, idiot. Who did you think? The Queen Mother? See ya. Don't be late."

I arrived at the Tadich Grill at 8:15. If I was going to get lucky, I might as well do it on my own terms.

IN VINO, BULLSHIT

"HOW'S THE QUARTER looking, Egon?" asked Jacob tentatively, sweat now streaming off his pasty brow. It was about sixty-five in the gloomy, grimy, venerable San Francisco eatery.

"WTF, dude?" asked Egon despairingly. Then turning to Barry, "Who are these d-bags you've got here tonight, Bazza? What a group of losers."

Barry glared at Jacob, who looked like he was about to choke on the mountain of fish he had nonchalantly dumped in his gob after dropping his latest bombshell.

"Haven't they heard of Reg FD? You know I can't answer that."

I was pleased that he at least had some idea of securities law.

Before Barry had a chance to intervene, Egon had grabbed a sourdough roll and thrown it at Jacob. It landed slap in the face of the guy in the wheelchair, who couldn't get his arms up to defend himself.

"Fuck, sorry, dude," Egon apologized. "Never was a very good pitcher; more of a catcher." The room erupted in nervous laughter. Egon took off his mirrored shades. I noticed his pupils were the size of quarters. "Actually, the quarter's going great if you must know, Jabba." Furious scribbling from the assembled party of twelve, save me.

"But don't quote me on that." Furious scribbling.

"I said don't quote me." Furious scribbling.

"Will you have revenue?" asked Charlton Heston. It wasn't Charlton, of course. He was dead somewhere, with his cold hands on an AR-15, presumably. It was the man in the wheelchair speaking through a computerized system that he tapped on with surprising dexterity. I found out later that rumor had it he had ALS, and was the only person crazy enough to still be short the stock after Fin covered. At least that's what Tom said.

"Fuck no." Egon giggled maniacally. "Why would I want fucking revenue? Revenue anchors people to numbers. Numbers are bullshit. Ideas are what matter. With ideas you have limitless opportunity; with numbers you have a model. Models are bullshit, so why have revenue?"

Someone nodded sagaciously. So everyone nodded sagaciously. Silence. Apparently, no one knew where to go from here. Barry looked frustrated.

This was my chance; I needed to get into the conversation. Though I'd been sitting to Egon's right for well over an hour now, I'd done little more than say hello. He hadn't responded.

"What will the planet look like when you've solved climate change?" I mumbled. It was the worst question I'd ever asked, but it was the first that came to mind, largely, I assume, because it was so cold in the restaurant and I'd forgotten my POS fleece. It was also the question that changed my life.

"Who's this fucking genius?" shouted Egon at the ceiling.

"I'm so sorry, Egon," Barry chimed in. Everyone looked at me as though I was a heroin addict in the Tenderloin. "He's new. I don't even know his name."

"He's a fucking genius, more like," answered Egon, swiveling on his chair and noticing me for the first time, apparently. He gave me a huge slap on the back. The scoop of Dungeness crab I had been laboriously masticating ejected onto his black T-shirt (he had changed from business casual to formal for the dinner by slipping a T-shirt on under his fur vest). He swatted it off with panache.

"At last someone has asked a fucking relevant question. Perhaps the best I've ever heard from one of you dumbasses. Who is this genius for real, Barry?"

"Giles, one of our veteran superstars," replied Barry without the slightest hesitation. "He's covered you since day one, and has always had a buy rating on the stock." It seems he knew more about me than I could possibly have imagined.

"Certain Buy," I stated proudly, as happy now as one of Tadich's clams (before it had been steamed alive).

"Certain By…being fucking right," continued Egon, clearly impressed with his pun. "That's exactly what people should be asking." He put his hand on my thigh. It seemed appropriate.

"What's your price target, guru?"

"Fifty percent above today's price." I beamed.

"But the stock is up thirty percent in the aftermarket," castigated Egon.

"Fifty percent above that then," I suggested. "Based on my updated model," I added quickly.

"That will do for now," he approved. "You have seen the fucking light." He sighed. "And now to answer your question, Jill. The world is going to be at peace, brothers," he said with a hum, closing his eyes and adopting a yogic position, his hands together in prayer. "The world is going to be at peace."

Silence. I looked around. Everyone had closed their eyes.

It was Silicon Valley's answer to The Last Supper, though Jesus never recited poetry (I think. Does anyone actually know?). Egon did, in a quiet, plaintiff murmur.

"I wandered lonely as a cloud
That floats on high o'er vales and hills,
When all at once I saw a crowd,
A host, of golden daffodils;
Beside the lake, beneath the trees,
Fluttering and dancing in the breeze."

Silence from the disciples. The rest of the restaurant rudely clattered on.

"Open your fucking eyes," implored Egon. Everyone did. Mine had never closed.

"Metaphorically, you morons," shouted Egon, loving every moment. Half the room closed their eyes again. The others looked scared. Half of that half then closed theirs. Then the rest, apart from Charlton.

"There won't be any more daffodils, lakes, or trees with you moneychangers in control. You are a bunch of bloodsucking leeches, only interested in your next dollar. You know nothing of the beauty of the universe, the inevitability of human progress, the feeling of omniscience, the aura of fucking genius. I know. Zyxview knows. Go back to your holes, spawns of Satan, be gone." Egon threw his glass of Lafite at Jacob. It smashed on the rim of Charlton's wheelchair.

I burst into applause. It was genuine. Everyone else burst into applause. Egon hugged me. It was beautiful. The rest of the restaurant paid us no attention.

"Any more questions?" asked Barry finally, when the confused elation had subsided.

"Are you going to hit your numbers this year?" asked an Asian fellow to Egon's left.

"Judas!" screamed Egon, leaping to his feet.

I heard Dipak was let go the following week. I felt for him. At least he had had the decency not to blow my cover.

QUO VADIS, JILL?

TEN BOTTLES OF Lafite later, everyone began to depart. Egon was the first up and first out. I tried to hand him my business card as he left, but he merely gave me knuckles and a playful punch to the stomach. I guess I had at least asked a question, though I doubted that would qualify as the edge Peter was looking for.

"Nice work, Giles," said Barry, chugging the last hundred dollars out of his wineglass. "I need to bring you to more of these. See you in the office?"

"I'll be around for sure," I answered enigmatically, and made a beeline for the door. It took me a while to get there, as Charlton had caused a minor traffic jam.

⤸

Now that it was nighttime, San Francisco had warmed up considerably. The layer of fog had been replaced by clouds. I tripped over an invisible heroin user and picked my way toward my hotel through the heaps of trash and prostrate bodies. I felt like a scout sent out to survey a medieval battle-field after a particularly bloody day of lancing.

I also felt like shit. I couldn't really blame the Lafite, though I couldn't rule out that it was actually Gallo jug wine (oldest trick in the book). It was more likely my failure to achieve anything meaningful with Egon, or anything meaningful at all. But then did anything have meaning when death could come at any moment?

I was ready to go back to New York and resign. Having witnessed Egon in action, I was somewhat relieved, to be honest, that I wasn't going to be getting any more involved in his circus, let alone getting to know him on any kind of personal level.

"All is for the best." I replayed my mother's favorite and final maxim over and over again, set incongruously to "Silent Night." It was the only lullaby I remember her singing. It may have been the only one she knew. It still comforted me all these years later.

I was jolted from my half-hearted existential crisis by a recently familiar voice.

"D-bag, get in."

I looked up to see a black stretch Hummer pulling up next to me unnoticed, like a lion stalking its prey. Its engine purred menacingly. And the back-back window was down. As I crouched to investigate, the door swung open. Inside was Egon.

"Get in quickly, Jill."

"Giles."

"Get in, Jill."

I did as I was told. I suppose my English education kicked in again, or was it my German stepmother's doing? Obedience had been spanked into me, either way.

"Drive, Bill."

And with that, I was next to Egon, in a limo, heading somewhere on a starry night (courtesy of the interior ceiling of the limo). I immediately noticed he had changed out of formal and back into business casual (he had removed the T-shirt from under his fur vest).

"You may wonder why you are here and where we are going, Einstein," said Egon, pouring us large drinks from the decanters that lined the sides, and taking two large sniffs from something in his pocket. I didn't mention that I hadn't been wondering that at all. I was now. "You are here for no reason and we are going nowhere," he went on, draining his tumbler with a swig and refilling it simultaneously. "Cheers."

I clinked his glass and took a cautious sip. Whisky. Not bad actually. Probably a rare Macallan (I had drunk my fair share at the Bullingdon). Class in a glass is better than no class at all, I guess.

"Look, princess, I don't usually do this." I wasn't sure. It seemed exactly like something he would do. "But I like you. I like you a lot."

I think he gazed into my eyes; but as he had his mirrored shades back on, I couldn't be certain. It was highly unlikely he could see anything, so perhaps I was imagining it. I didn't imagine the hand he placed on my thigh again. His voice had a different tone. I might have called it sultry if I'd been able to concentrate. After a long pause, he backed off a bit.

"The question you asked tonight was the worst fucking question I have ever been asked."

"Thank you," I demurred.

"But as you asked it, I suddenly realized that you weren't asking that question. You were asking the best fucking question I've ever been asked."

"I was?!" I was caught between a question and a statement. I'm not sure it came across that way.

"Stop acting dumb. You're safe in here." I didn't feel the

slightest bit safe. "What you were asking was why I am such a fucking genius."

"I was?!" I continued to hedge. I was a good deal better at hedging responses than stocks. That much I knew. And I was lousy at the former, apparently.

"Stop asking questions. You know that's exactly what you meant."

"Okay." That seemed suitably concrete.

"That's right. I'm a fucking genius. And you may be the first person to fully realize it."

"I doubt that, Egon." I tried to avoid eye contact—with myself in his mirrored lenses. I turned to the window. That didn't work as it achieved the same effect. So I looked at the shag carpeting.

"Don't be so bashful." He laughed with a sudden explosion, punching me hard on the shoulder. I was going to have some explaining to do with Cherry. I would be black and blue by the morning at this rate. I'd have to pretend Jamie got nasty with me.

"Only true geniuses recognize genius in others," he continued, simmering down. "You see, Jillian, when I started Zyxview I had no idea what I was doing." That wasn't what I had written in my initiation on the stock, but then I suppose I'd had no idea what I was doing either. I still don't, as you've realized if you've read this far. "I knew I had a concept, which had always been enough. I sold AppApp on that basis for half a bill."

"Yes, sir." It appeared the mention of "bill" had stirred the silhouette of a driver.

"Not you, Bill. What are you, a fucking detective? Stop listening, and drive."

"Yes, sir."

"I said stop listening, d-bag." Egon reached over to a switch that closed a screen, separating Bill from us. That was not a development I had been hoping for.

"Anyway, so when I sold AppApp for half a bill, I had an awakening. If I could sell that piece of shit for three commas, imagine what I could sell a real company for." (There were several lawsuits still pending.)

"A lot," I proffered stupidly.

"Exactly. You *are* a genius. A lot of a lot. Four commas at the very least."

"That's a trillion dollars."

"No shit, Sherlock. Stop interrupting me. I'm about to tell you everything."

"Before you do, Egon," I interjected, "please don't tell me anything material or non-public. I don't want to have to restrict myself on the stock." There it was. I'd got it out of my system just in time, in a very courteous and professional manner, I thought proudly.

"What the fuck, dude? How rude! I thought you were a genius investor, not some amateur schoolgirl. Do you think I'd tell you anything I shouldn't? What do you take me for, a criminal? A charlatan? I've got a good mind to kick you right out onto the street. Tell me why I shouldn't."

"Sorry, Egon. I was just trying to protect you," I lied.

"You're the one who's going to need protection from my fucking fist if you don't shut up. Act like you're as smart as you seemed."

"Okay." I accepted the humiliation willingly, almost thankfully.

"So…*anyways*…I decided to set up Zyxview. But all I had was a concept. Admittedly, it was a fucking genius concept. I was going to set up a company that solved everything." That much I knew; it was all over their SEC filings. "But what was I going to solve? What was everything?"

He was clearly waiting for a response.

"I don't know."

That wasn't the response he'd been looking for.

"Giles, if we're going to get along, you have to stop acting as dumb as those other d-bags at the dinner. You're better than that."

"I am?"

"Fuck I hope so, or this is going to be an even shorter ride than I'd planned. Last chance or you'll be hanging with the rats in the gutter. What is everything?"

I was stumped, so I retreated to that last vestige of presumed intelligence, my classical education. "I did have a professor once," I began cautiously, "who told me that everything is nothing because *nihil ex nihilo*. Nothing can come from nothing. And if nothing can, then everything certainly can't. At least I think that's what he said."

"Dude, you've gone way under my head there. But if what you are trying to say is that everything is whatever I think it is, then you are spot-on."

"Exactly."

"Good. We are getting somewhere. So I realized that whatever I decided to solve was everything that needed to be solved."

"Brilliant."

"I know. It was like a flash of inspiration."

"That required no perspiration," I joked half-heartedly, happy that I was still in the car.

"That required you to shut the fuck up, brosepher." I shut up again. "Global warming, income inequality, hatred, war, plagues, jock itch, in fact any sort of fungus-generated chafing you can imagine, you name it, I would have an answer to it because I had a question about it." I remained shut up. "What do you think?"

"You're solving jock itch?" I asked tentatively.

"Nope. That is what is called an example, Edison. I'm solving nothing."

"Nothing?"

"Which is everything."

"Everything."

"You're getting it, now. It's epic. By not actually solving anything, I'm solving everything. And the VCs loved it when I pitched it to them."

"The VCs?"

"You know, venture capitalists, aka that group of self-impressed tagnuts that hang out on Sand Hill Road. The ones that invest in the early stage companies that everyone else is investing in, without having a clue what they are doing."

"Well, they've certainly done pretty well, what with Google, Apple, Netflix, and so on," I suggested contrarily.

"Bull-fucking-shit," shouted Egon. "One or two of them have gotten lucky with one or two of their investments. The rest stank. Unfortunately, that rest accounts for about 99.9 percent of what the industry as a whole has done. Net-net they've made about five dollars between them."

I did remember reading an article by mistake in the *Wall Street Journal* once about how Calpers had pulled out of VC funds as they had returned less than index funds. I'd dismissed it as classic journalistic envy (which it probably was).

"What about all those Atherton mansions then," I asked timidly.

"Oh yeah, I meant to say they've made about five dollars *for their investors*. A lot of them personally have made fortunes. Actually, maybe they are smarter than I give them credit for. But that's not the point."

"What is the point?"

"Nothing. Nothing's the point. That's why they invested in Zyxview. When I told them that my idea for a company was one that solved everything, they hesitated. When I told them it had no product yet, they were enthused. Sequoia got on board. So everyone got on board. They couldn't help but throw money at me. That's even why I called it Zyxview. It's just the end of the alphabet reversed. ZYXWVU. Perfect for a company without a product."

I wondered briefly if that was inside information. No, it was pretty irrelevant, I deemed, though interesting. Certainly, having covered the stock for a decade, I hadn't given much thought to its name. Nor had anyone else as far as I knew, though there was an analyst in the early days who had asked in a research note "what is Zyxview, what does it even mean?" I'd never heard from him again. Then his price target was only 10 percent above the closing price, so it wasn't surprising that he was fired. What's worse, his rating, if I recall correctly, had only been "accumulate," whatever that means.

"So are you saying Zyxview doesn't have a product?!" Another hedge.

"I never said that. I couldn't. I just said that's why the VCs invested when we were a private company. You may conclude whatever you like about the current state of affairs, but I never said anything about it, matey. That's non-public information, Mr. SEC."

He was right, of course. His equivocation had saved me from my own foolish question-statement. He hadn't said anything. He certainly had said nothing though. Several times. So I was still in the clear. "You can only assume what is public information, gorgeous, and no more: that we are still looking at everything."

"That seems like a reasonable assumption."

"So the upside potential is still limitless," he stated gleefully.

"Limitless," I repeated, like he was playing a Jedi mind-trick on me.

"Infinite in fact. Everything and nothing, merging as one at the ends of time." With that he chased the rest of his whisky and topped us both up.

"The thing is, sweetheart, that it's the story of my life. I've always been everything, and I've always been nothing. That's why I beat up Chanel." His contretemps with his current Victoria's Secret model girlfriend you've already heard about. "She just didn't understand me. I'm not sure she understood anything." He was right about that, I suspected.

His sudden moroseness was more unnerving than his prior mania. I almost suggested he take another sniff of whatever was in his pocket to perk him up. Wisely, I only almost suggested it. It might have killed him.

"You see, my mother died when I was young."

"Mine too."

"Really?" he asked, removing his shades and sidling up closer to me. This time his bloodshot eyes were definitely gazing into mine. I was transfixed, I'll admit. Could eyes really be that bloodshot and still see? His pupils were the size of silver dollars.

"Yes, she died of ALS when I was six," I said soberly.

"Are you fucking kidding me? So did mine," he choked.

"Of ALS?"

"No, in a freak trapeze accident while in her usual alcoholic stupor. But I was six."

"It sucks, doesn't it," I said, trying to find an appropriate end to this tack in the conversation.

"It sure does, man," said Egon, beginning to cry. "After that nothing means anything. Yet it means everything too. I wanted to be something for her, to achieve something she couldn't."

"Sobriety?" I suggested flippantly, trying desperately to lighten the mood.

"No fucking way, Giles." The use of my correct name was disconcerting. "Alcoholism was the best thing she had going for her. No, I wanted to achieve something special. And the only way to do that, to be special in America, is to become stupendously rich."

"Well, cheer up, you've achieved that and so much more," I partly lied.

"No I haven't," said Egon glumly. "You're such a sweetheart to say it, but I haven't. I am a genius, but I'm only a billionaire. That's like nothing. I need to be a trillionaire to really get somewhere. Not that it matters, as she's dead."

"But no one's a trillionaire, not even Gates, Bezos, or Buffett," I said, trying to cheer him up. It didn't work.

"Exactly, dude. Not even MacKenzie-fucking-Bezos. It's so sad. I feel for her." He was sobbing again. "And I'm so fucking scared I'm not going to get there. I'm so scared that if I announce a product, the stock will tank."

"Why?"

"Because if I have a product, I can't be solving everything, I must be solving something. And something's worth nowhere near as much as everything. It may even be worth less than nothing."

"Sounds like it." I wasn't helping, but logic demanded it.

"What should I do then? I've spent years developing this business model."

"Well, I don't know that you actually have a product, so perhaps there is nothing to worry about."

"Absolutely. You know nothing. But hypothetically, let's assume that despite my best efforts I had a product that was going change the entire world as we know it."

"You do?"

"You know I can't tell you that," said Egon, frustrated at my slip.

"Of course. My bad. But say you did, hypothetically. What would it be like?"

"It would be fucking incredible. A peach. Change the world. But it wouldn't change everything, and that's the problem."

"What a disaster," I concluded, getting where he was going. I thought long and hard for about a second. "I just wouldn't announce it then, if you hypothetically were to have it. And I wouldn't launch its hypothetical ass, either." I thought descending to his level of humor might cheer him up.

"But I would have to, honey, I wouldn't have a choice," he said, putting his hand back on my thigh. My sphincter began to pucker. Ever since boarding school it's been my autonomous reaction to fear. I'll leave you to guess why.

"Why would you have to?" I asked, intrigued.

"Because everyone who works for me would quit if they were to think we didn't have a product, and the company would collapse. Time would be running out. People would be getting agitated."

"But everyone who owns Zyxview would sell if they thought you had a product that doesn't solve everything," I observed, cottoning on to his logic. "Which would result in the company collapsing if you were to run out of capital, and then everyone who works for you would quit anyway."

"Exactly."

I suddenly realized it. In this hypothetical scenario, we were both screwed. I hoped reality was different. But then what did *I* know?

"That's why I pulled you into my limo. Your question proved you're the only person smart enough to work a way out of this catch-22. Because you're the only person who knows why my genius has gotten me into this situation."

"Because you've hypothetically overdelivered on your promise to do nothing by hypothetically doing something, and thereby hypothetically not doing everything."

"Eureka."

"Eurekas, I think you mean." I couldn't help myself.

"Ass is right. Ass-fucked is what I am. Though that's not all bad," he continued with a wink. Or it may have been a blink.

"That's what my wife tells me." I laughed. Facetiousness was the last weapon in my armory of humor. We had reached a nadir.

"So what's my way out, Solomon?"

I had nothing. Nothing. Which was less than everything but more than something, I think. Then it hit me. Call it fate, call it karma, or call it luck. Actually, just call it luck.

"Eureka," I exploded.

"Or -ass?" he asked, genuinely.

"In this case no '-ass' involved. I've got it. If this hypothetical product were to exist, I wouldn't make an announcement."

"Is that the fucking best you've got? Haven't we just been there?"

"Yes, but I would make an *announcement*."

"What the fuck? What do you mean? You said you wouldn't." The genius was stumped.

"I would make an announcement…that you are going to be making an announcement about something. At some unspecified point in the future. Not too far out to be worrying, but not too soon to cause panic. And keep doing that until you come up with a better idea."

Egon was dumbstruck. I knew that because he stopped talking for fifteen seconds.

"You are a fucking genius. I knew it."

"Thank you," I said, stunned by my *coup de grâce*. "All is for the best. That's what my mom used to say."

"I love it, man. All *is* for the best. What a fucking great saying. And I love you too. I want to kiss you. I want to make love to you. I want your eu-reek-ass."

"Sorry, Egon, I'm not gay," I replied. I thought it was time to confess this to him from a position of strength as it were, before his hand, which had begun riding my abductor toward my crotch, reached its destination. Despite wanting to be gay (mostly to piss my father off), or at least bisexual (to increase my options), I'd found from a few near misses that I wasn't either. That said, I love gay men on all other dimensions than love. After all, they are the only men with an EQ above a Neanderthal. As for gay women, I have been lucky enough to love some of them on every dimension, though I guess that makes them bisexual. Let's just leave it at that.

"Nor am I, dude," Egon shot back surprisingly, withdrawing and shifting to the other side of the car. "No fucking way."

"Of course not. Not that there is anything wrong with being gay."

"Nope, no dude's Hershey Highway for this rabid heterosexual," he said, distractedly, gazing into space. "Nope. But an announcement of an announcement…" he mused under his breath. "Of course, so simple. A genius would never think of that."

He took another sniff from his pocket. I was relieved. So was he clearly, as he jumped up and banged on the screen separating us from Bill.

"There is a button for that, sir," said Bill flatly.

"I know there's a fucking button for that," chided Egon. "Thanks for your insight, Miss Marple. Take me to where I'm going, and then take my best friend to his hotel."

"Certainly, sir. We have arrived." Bill was unlikely to be a clairvoyant (though I couldn't rule anything out this evening), so I clung to the logic this wasn't an unexpected destination.

"Hasta la vista, baby," said Egon, jumping out and slamming the door behind as fast as he could. It didn't work. I got a peek of the Castro Street sign as clear as day.

"And for you, sir?"

"The Mandarin Oriental, please," I pleaded, as I closed the screen on Bill.

VARIUM ET MUTABILE
SEMPER FEMINA

THE CAB RIDE home was particularly unpleasant, and
that's saying something given the state of most New York
taxis. But I hadn't bothered learning how to use Uber or Lyft.
I wasn't a techie, remember, just a tech "investor." In any case,
my spirits were so high that I almost commended the driver
on his BO, and did congratulate him for not having working
air-conditioning. For once in my life I'd exceeded my expecta-
tions. It wasn't hard, as I'd always set them pretty low—which
tells you all you need to know about my performance. In
celebration, I doubled the driver's tip.

I knew more than everything I needed or wanted to know
about Egon and Zyxview, without having broken the law.
He'd never told me anything about the company (nothing
couldn't be something, right?), and any upcoming announcement of an announcement wasn't inside information. It was
my idea in response to a hypothetical scenario he had laid
out. And no reasonable investor could have a clue whether he
would follow my advice. Having met all of Zyxview's reasonable investors, I knew that for sure, as they didn't have a clue
about anything, let alone nothing in particular.

All was one hundred percent absolutely and unconditionally for the best.

⤙

My Panglossian mood was further titillated by Cherry. Not only was she waiting for me naked (not unusual, to be fair). She had news. I could tell that because she was typing on her iPhone. She never typed unless she was sharing something big, as it was a slow process. She shared a lot. But she rarely shared something big, as she rarely typed.

"We're pregnant!" she screamed, hitting me in the face with her 36DDs as she jumped into my arms. I nuzzled and gurgled. It was instinctive, as you know. You would have too, to be honest, whether you are a man, woman, or something in between. They were a work of art (almost literally; her plastic surgeon had won several awards as a sculpturist).

"We are?!" My surprise was genuine. We had agreed not to have babies for several years, though I knew she wanted at least five (she was a breeder, she said, and besides, they pictured so well for Instagram). I thought one or two might be more prudent. I used climate change as my excuse. Who would want to raise too many kids in a world where there might not be enough dry land for them? She understood, she said (she followed Al Gore on Twitter). I anticipated at least four.

In the meantime, Cherry had claimed to have had an IUD inserted. I suggested to match her DUI. She didn't get it. We usually used condoms too, having grown into the habit from our earliest dating. She had been paranoid that uncircumcised men carried AIDS, and I had been fortunate enough to avoid the snip after a last-minute intervention from my father, who had been less fortunate (the "heathen" exploits of a trigger-happy Jewish doctor, he claimed).

"Yes, we sure are, honey!" she confirmed. "I missed a couple of periods, and the doc says I'm at least two months in. I took my IUD out to stop the acne I was getting." I hadn't noticed any. "I'm sorry I didn't tell you. I just didn't think it would all happen so fast. Are you mad?"

"No, of course not. That's wonderful news, sweetheart. Who's the father?"

"You're so funny. That's why I married you. I hope all our babies are as funny as their daddy." I knew five was back on the table.

We celebrated the tidings as Cherry dictated. One hour in bed, followed by an hour-long Instagram shoot. I tried my best to look elated for the selfies. Not that I wasn't. I just wasn't photogenic. Perhaps trying was the problem.

"I invited your daddy and Helga over for champagne," she said after posting.

"How sweet of you. What time are they coming to judge?"

"Don't be sarcastic," she implored. After five years, she had begun to recognize irony, though hadn't advanced far enough to use it. I didn't want to rush her. There are some nasty side effects.

"They really love you," she continued.

"*Really,* as in a lot or despite all appearances?"

"Whatever," she said, as grumpily as she ever got.

"I'm kidding," I lied.

"Just give them a chance. They are good people."

"They aren't all bad, it's true," I said, as quixotically as I knew how. "In any case, nothing can spoil our happiness. It's been an amazing week. I had an amazing meeting with Egon too. Everything is going swimmingly." I spared her the details.

"That's great news. Did he like you?"

"Perhaps too much."

"That's impossible." She smiled. "No one can like you too much because you're like perfect." I smiled back. She didn't need to know the whole story.

"Oh shucks, I've gotta run now. I'm late for my Pilates," she said suddenly in a panic. "Hector will kill me. He says we need every second of our session to keep my six-pack toned. I'm fighting time, he says."

"And a baby doing its worst from the inside."

"Oh gosh, I hadn't thought about that. I'm just going to need to work for two." I suspected she didn't know you couldn't maintain a six-pack with a balloon in your abdomen, but I didn't want to be the bearer of bad tidings. Shooting the messenger, and all that. Nothing would ruin my perfect day.

When she left, I sat on the sofa and tried to take everything in. I couldn't explain it, but I was worried. Things were going too well. Zyxview was up another 10 percent. Peter had rung to congratulate me. Egon was my friend now. I was going to be a father. What couldn't go wrong?

As I adjusted my underwear and made myself a Nespresso, I decided that I needed to go for a jog to clear my head. Going to the office would be inviting catastrophe.

∽

I had only made it as far as 72nd and 5th when my music cut out. My phone was ringing. 650-123-3210. Palo Alto. Interesting number. So I picked up.

"Hey, d-bag." It was unmistakably Egon's voice.

"Hey, man, how are you? I had a great time the other evening. What can I do for you?"

"I never, ever want to hear from you again."

Maybe I should have kissed him.

"Okay, but Egon…" He had already hung up.

Fuck. I walked home listening religiously to one of my dad's favorites, *Carmina Burana*. "*O fortuna, velut luna, statu variabilis…*" It seemed appropriate. I have a flair for melodramatic self-pity.

GERMANIA

MY FATHER AND Helga arrived at six sharp. Their promptness never ceased to piss me off. To be fair, given my mood, I would have been even more pissed if they'd been late.

Andrew Roman Goodenough IV was a consequential individual. He had terrified me from my earliest memories. It probably went even further back than that. I was born two months premature. He most likely scared me out of my mother, before scarring me for life. I remember as a kid that all I wanted to do was impress him. I gave up trying by the time I was sent to board at St. Paul's School, London.

"How is your new job going? In trouble yet?" my father asked when I opened the door. It was as if his misanthropy had endowed him with telepathy. "I'd suggest you accelerate your path to riches, Giles, or you'll run out of time to do something valuable with your life. Remember, money is a means to an end, not an end itself. Not that you've ever listened to me. *Abite nummi, ego vos mergam, ne mergar a vobis.* Don't let your greed control you." That was easy for him to say. The trust fund had been larger before he'd started getting involved with it.

He was born in 1955 to the famed (in our family) turkey-stuffing entrepreneur, Andrew Goodenough III. Vadoma, his mother, was a Gypsy who had charmed "Good Old Drew" in every way at a local fair, hence my father's middle name (he claimed it was in honor of Caesar). He was educated at St. Paul's (New Hampshire), Groton, Harvard, and Oxford. Need I say more? For your sakes, I will force myself.

A brilliant classicist (I stumbled ineptly far behind his mammoth tracks), he had a penchant for wine and youth. He "transferred out" of St. Paul's after being caught with the rector's daughter ("it was under the lord's table, *mea culpa,*" "better than being caught with the daughter's rectum," "she was almost fifteen, what do you expect?" and so on—you get the drift). He graduated Harvard *summa cum laude*, and then took seven years at Oxford to write his PhD (foxhunting having interfered with the finer points of Tacitus's *Germania*, apparently). That's where he met my mother. She was also the daughter of a minister, albeit an Irish Catholic priest. I will reluctantly applaud him for his consistency. And at least she was eighteen. Just. And as sweet as he was sour.

I followed not long after, disappointingly early. It was the first of many disappointments, he has often told me. I wasn't tall enough, blond enough, or bright enough.

He rectified the lacuna generated by my insufficiency soon after my mother's death by marrying Helga. She was a German student, studying under him at Columbia (apparently all too literally), where he had reluctantly relocated us for the better money (or "to teach Americans their culture," as he invariably claimed). She was tall, blonde, and bright. She was also twenty-four. So he was making progress, in a manner.

Nor was she a rector's daughter. Her father had been a champagne salesman like his father, who, she proudly admitted when drunk on champagne, had been best pals with (von) Ribbentrop ("wouldn't hurt a fly") and personal sommelier to

Hitler and Goering (better business coming no doubt from the latter). "He was absolutely not a Nazi," she emphasized, though her disavowal, it seemed, stemmed more from an inherited detestation of their poor taste and uncouth manners than the seventy million they left dead in their wake.

Beyond that, she was surprisingly funny for a German. She occasionally even told a joke. She and my father raised me efficiently after my mother's death. There wasn't a lot of love, but then I wasn't her child, and at least she spared me half-siblings. As a couple they were rarely amusing, never comprehensible (I only knew she was joking when she laughed). And she fitted my father's cultivated prejudices perfectly.

He was convinced, you see, of the inherent superiority of the Teutonic race (if there is such a thing), and had the arrogance to believe he had discovered its purest form. "It is right there in *Germania*," he said. He also believed that the Batavians had been Celts—no doubt how he brought himself to marry my redheaded and freckled mother (that and the pregnancy, perhaps). But that's by the by. Suffice to say that together my father's and Helga's egos bestrode this narrow world like Colossi, leaving all us petty men peeping about them (my father used to recite *Julius Caesar* to me at bedtime. That fragment alone stuck). I fortunately inherited none of my father's prejudices (that I could tell—or perhaps I just inherited some of my mother's love of everything and everyone). I did inherit his taste in women, I'll confess.

I never had it in me to tell my father that he was, in fact, mostly Jewish and Gypsy. Okay, to be precise, 30 percent Jewish, 30 percent Balkan (i.e., Romani, i.e., Gypsy), 30 percent British, and 10 percent other (perhaps the most interesting discovery, the possibilities were delicious). That had to be the case as I'd done 23andMe out of boredom, and

I was certain my mother accounted for at least 50 percent of my 65 percent British-Irish genome (there wasn't much confusion for the Murphys). Like most good Americans he was a purebred mutt. It would have destroyed him to find out. When I say I never had it in me to tell him, I'll be honest. I was just waiting for the right moment.

"Congratulations, children," he patronized on entry. "At least one new child unlikely to be on welfare will be a great boon for this nation." That was a weak opener if he'd been rehearsing it.

"Thank you, pater," I slurred.

"I see you have already been celebrating," said Helga, judging immediately. She was right. I was moderately (English) pissed, having pre-gamed sufficient Krug to at least waterboard my sorrows by late afternoon. Cherry had barely noticed (she had been on Instagram since 2 p.m.).

"It's five o'clock somewhere," I riffed.

"Well, it's six o'clock here," stated Helga with a laugh and a cough.

"Very good, Helga," I scoffed, apparently too blatantly.

"That's quite enough from you, boy." *Boy* was not his worst pejorative. He was clearly in a pretty good mood, for him.

"Sorry, Father."

"And where is my beautiful farm girl?" he continued, satisfied at my lukewarm apology.

"Here I am, Dad!" Cherry cantered in gleefully and threw herself in my father's arms. Her breasts hit him in the face. He didn't nuzzle. But he did blush.

"Such comely pulchritude, a true Venus," he added, looking her up and down as she unlocked from him. Helga frowned. "You are *fecundissima*. Sadly, it looks like my son got there first." Helga coughed loudly. It sounded physical rather than simply judgmental. It could have been either, or both.

"I sure am!" Cherry laughed. She didn't have a clue what he was talking about, of course. "Come on, let's pop the pop."

"Pop *ze* pop," I repeated lavishly. "*Jawohl, mein fuehrer.*" I clicked my heels and went to the fridge, pursued by disapproving clicking from Helga's tongue. I was furious at the Egon situation, and was taking it out on them—they would have done the same or worse in my position.

We all took our seats opposite each other on the sofas and gazed out of the window onto the hubbub of Third Avenue. Our apartment was smallish and garish (thanks to Cherry), and there was really nowhere better to gaze. We clinked our glasses and went through the motions of small talk, a challenge for my father, whose banter was usually Wagnerian in scale and scope.

I only remember a smattering of the conversation. It wasn't particularly enlightening, and I won't bore you with much. I was more than tipsy, and couldn't help obsessing over Egon's call (which was especially disconcerting as I rarely obsess about anything other than death). Perhaps it didn't matter that he'd cut off all ties? After all, the announcement of an announcement may still come. I could survive on that. Or was it coming? If it did, I could get Peter to sell the entire position in the ensuing euphoria and call it a year. If it didn't, then surely momentum would continue "up and to the right." Or was this the turning point, the denouement, or the catastrophe? Was there a difference? What was it?

"I'll get my mother to tell you the secret to her geraniums," said Cherry at one point.

"Germania?" I asked, awoken from my meditations. I was clueless as to the conversation.

"Either will do," said Helga.

"I think geraniums is preferable," my father interjected. "Sufficiently Anglicized at this stage, surely?"

"I said Ger-mania," I garbled insistently. No one paid me any attention, which was a pity as that had been my weightiest contribution to this point. More persiflage. A little later Helga had a coughing fit, which I rectified with a glass of brandy. And then, soon after, I think, they departed, but not before insisting we consider Hans as a name for the baby, it being both Helga and Cherry's fathers' name. No one openly considered that it might be a girl. Other than providence, perhaps.

"Helga doesn't sound well, baby," said Cherry with genuine concern, when the door had closed firmly behind them.

"Oh, don't worry about her," I said dismissively. "She smoked like a bonfire till a year or two ago, as you know. Perhaps her lungs are just on strike over poor historical working conditions... Or perhaps she is dying."

"Oh lord, I hope not."

"I'm joking, honey."

"Well, it's not like very funny, Giles." The use of my name meant she was about as angry with me as she ever got. "What is wrong with you? Why have you been drinking all day? It's just not like you to be such a meanie." She was right, I rarely cared enough to be mean.

"I've had a bad day at work," I said meekly.

"But you didn't even go to work."

"I got a nasty call after you left for Pilates."

"Oh gee, what a bummer," she said, falling for my self-pity. "Are you sure this is the right job for you? You've been acting weird ever since you joined that place."

"It's only been a few weeks."

"Well, it's a few weeks too long as far as I'm concerned. Do I need to go over there and spank that naughty Peter guy?"

I laughed out loud. She knew exactly how to cheer me up. Perhaps that's why I married her (plus the other reasons I have already explained).

"You know, I didn't marry you *just* for the money," she said with a wink. She was even honest in her protestations. God, I love that girl.

"I know," I said hopefully.

"So come on, buckaroo. Let's go out and celebrate. My girls are so excited to see you, *Daddy*."

"Enough for group sex?"

"If you ask nicely," she only half joked.

WATERBOARDING

THE ANNOUNCEMENT CAME the following Monday before the market opened. It wasn't the announcement I'd been looking for. It wasn't even the announcement of an announcement I'd been looking for. And it certainly wasn't hypothetical. I immediately thought about resigning.

PALO ALTO—Business Wire—Zyxview (Nasdaq: ZYX) announces departure of Chief Engineering Officer Winston Chang.

"Who the fuck is Winston Chang?" demanded Peter from his yacht somewhere off St. Tropez (why he bothered going there I don't know, as he appeared to be trading all day—perhaps he wanted a change of air-conditioning).

"I'm not sure," I replied timidly. "I think he is part of their Chinese R&D center." I didn't know if they had a Chinese R&D center. But it sounded plausible.

"You're frickin' kidding me," said Peter in anger. "What do you mean you're not sure? I thought you knew everything about this company."

"I don't know nothing about the company, it's true, but it doesn't extend to every employee. I do, however, know almost everything about the stock." My attempt at obfuscation was idiotic. It got Peter to pause though, which was its aim.

"Well, that's something, but not enough," he mused. "So what's the stock going to do?"

"Open about fifteen percent down," I said. It was down 15 percent in the pre-market. "No big deal. Buy some more," I said confidently.

"You don't sound confident. In fact you sound terrified. That's not what I need right now. I might sell some and buy it back later," he ruminated aloud. He was clearly focused on the long term, as he told his investors. "But this isn't good news."

"No, but it's not really bad news. After all, I don't think anyone knows who he is. I don't think anyone even knows they have a chief engineering officer."

"Shit, that's even worse. If people knew who he was, it wouldn't be so bad."

"I don't get it," I said, genuinely confused.

"God, I hate these rookies," shouted Peter, to no one in particular. "Look, Giles, if people knew they had a chief engineering officer called Winston Chang, this wouldn't be a big deal. The guy is probably some useless nobody doing nothing. But they now know they have a chief engineering officer. That is bad news. What are they engineering? Does this mean it's delayed? Worse still, does it mean it doesn't work? Worse still, why are they engineering something? That sounds like they are doing something. And if they are doing something, they are unlikely to be doing everything. Is this just the first domino? And even worse he's Chinese. So people are going to assume he's a genius. Losing somebody isn't good, but losing a Chinese genius is a fucking disaster."

His ability to unravel the quintessence of the situation was uncanny, and I was starting to understand how this worked. I wished I'd never left Merrill. How would I break it to Peter that I wanted to quit? I couldn't summon the courage. Perhaps I was hoping he'd fire me.

A little later the full press release came across the wires. It just repeated the same information but added a quote from Egon. "All of the team would like to thank Winston for his incredible work at Zyxview. He was an instrumental part of the team, without whom none of what we have achieved would have been possible. We wish him well in his future endeavors." The stock fell further. Peter called back.

"How's the Côte d'Azur?" I asked. I didn't really care. Nor did Peter apparently, as he dismissed my question with a groan.

"I'm buying more."

"Okay, but I wouldn't. Did you read in the press release that he was instrumental?"

"Exactly...Jill," he sighed. How come this bastardization of my name was on the tip of everyone's tongues? It had plagued me since preschool. "That's great news."

"Of course?!" I hedged.

Peter knew I didn't have a clue. "Look, now that people know that he achieved so much as an instrumental part of the team, they know three things they didn't before. First, that there is a team—so losing him can't be that bad. Second—that he was instrumental—which is code for useless. Third—that they have achieved something, but nothing specific, which is fantastic. That's a lot better than not knowing anything. In fact, net-net this is great news."

"Of course?!"

Peter was right. Apparently, he understood the markets, though it could have just been a good guess. The stock opened down 25 percent. By the end of the day, it was flat. Peter had bought more at the open so had made a ton off the intraday action and was nicely up for the day. I felt sorry for the guys who had sold to him down 25 percent. I suspected Fin might have re-entered their short position. And Grandma and Grandpa got screwed too. Cramer had come out negative before the open. But then isn't that the whole point of the stock market? Just more trickle-up. At least my job seemed safe for the time being. I wouldn't have to quit for at least another day.

"Great work today, Giles." Peter called after the market closed. I was highly appreciative of his magnanimity. "Let's just hope there aren't more departures. Look, I was thinking that perhaps you should come over to my place this weekend. I want to get to know you better and perhaps even teach you a thing or two."

"Sure," I said enthusiastically. An invitation to Peter's was a sure sign that I was doing something right, right? Perhaps I'd even last a couple more weeks.

"Oh, and bring that stripper wife of yours." Damn, I knew Holton wouldn't be able to keep his jockish mouth shut. "I want to see what assets *you've* got under management." He laughed somewhere between boyishly and lewdly. I didn't laugh back.

✦

I saw Holton in the mirrors later that day, skulking around Peter's empty desk. Reflection is a two-way phenomenon. I decided to confront him about Cherry, so headed down.

"I can't believe you told Peter my wife was a stripper," I said nonchalantly, having crept up behind him as quietly as I could. He jumped a little but soon regained his composure.

"Don't sneak up on me like that, dude."

"I wasn't sneaking. I didn't want to disturb you. You look engrossed in something."

"I'm not engrossed in anything," he said defensively. "And I didn't tell Peter your wife was a stripper. I told him your wife *is* a stripper."

His use of the present tense wasn't entirely inaccurate, as Cherry did still make the occasional guest appearance around town. Not that I thought he would have known that, though in retrospect it should have been obvious that he likely would have, given his obvious enthusiasm for titty bars. I just hope he tipped her.

"He seemed to know anyway, Giles," he went on.

"He did?"

"Peter knows everything."

"Still…" I said gravely, "there was no need for you to throw fuel on the fire."

"Sorry, I guess. How did it come up anyway?"

"He's invited us both over to his house this weekend."

"His castle, you mean? Poor you. You're fucked."

I guess I'd misunderstood the tone of Peter's invitation.

INTERVIEW AT XANADU

THE TURRETS PROJECTED as majestically above the tree-lined shore as Cherry's did above her bra.

"We're here," said the Lyft driver emphatically. We had used Cherry's account.

"Well, we should be *there*," I said, pointing at the castle on the other side of the cove. I'd checked out the pictures on the Internet. Peter's castle wasn't a well-kept secret.

"The app says this is where you are going," replied the driver, already cursing under his breath.

"It's okay, honey, we'll walk. I want some fresh air anyway," said Cherry appeasingly.

That was easier said than done. Crossing a cove is why man created boats. Walking around a cove is why man created boots. We had neither. At least we got a scenic tour of the Connecticut coastline, I guess, and some ticks, which I swiped off our legs in a panic.

"They're just ants, silly!" said Cherry.

"No, they are ticks," I pronounced. "And they carry Lyme disease, which can kill you." On further examination, I discovered they were ants, I'll admit. But you can never be too careful when death is lurking.

We finally found a path, which led to a path, which led to

another over a moat, which led to a gate. We rang the buzzer and a disjointed voice welcomed us to Xanadu. I was glad we had walked; it might have taken an hour to find our way with a car. Why god invented feet, doubtlessly.

The castle was only slightly less impressive than the 4k-drone footage had suggested. Which was impressive in itself. Xanadu, I read on Wikipedia, had been built by a robber baron in the early twentieth century, one of those quaint old fellows who forged an empire in steel off the backs of Europe's immigrant masses. Twenty-first-century techniques for stealing hoards of capital from the proletariat were far more sophisticated and required far less actual work, thanks to the financialization of just about everything (and the enduring power of stories about cheerleaders, as Holton had revealed).

I couldn't help but appreciate the original owner's sense of humor, whatever his name was (I've already forgotten). After all, what better way to laugh at one's workers than by forcing them to forge enough steel to build oneself a castle of stone?

And what a castle it was. There were German princes who would have blushed before their serfs at such a level of ostentation, even during their first great *Reich*, the Holy Roman one. The European Union had nothing so grand, despite the best efforts of the architects in Brussels and Strasbourg, at the direction of their masters in Berlin. I'll spare you all the details—the spires, the great halls, the labyrinthine staircases and corridors—as I have a story to tell. Suffice to say that at 100,000 square feet (or more, no one was sure), it was among the larger inhabited castles in the world. At least Peter had a flair for megalomania.

⮝

The lady who greeted us in the cavernous foyer was worse for wear. Of indeterminable age, she looked like a sixty-year-old high-class hooker (I'd seen more than a few at Annabel's). And though her dimensions corresponded roughly to Cherry's, it was clear that a plastic surgeon somewhere was fighting an uphill battle against nature's downhill momentum. Her face was as taut as the skin of a boiled tomato, and her lips like two giant petrified leeches. Her platinum blonde hair was mostly wig, I suspected.

She looked us up and down. "Hello, people," she said in a heavy Eastern European accent. "My name is Daria, Petr's vife, how are yours?"

I hoped I had translated her question correctly. "My name is Gi-les. This is Che-rry." I spoke so slowly that I sounded retarded (sorry, developmentally challenged—I always make that mistake, not from prejudice but habit). Cherry smiled politely though I could tell she was nervous, as she wasn't giggling nervously.

"Oh, is good meet you both," Daria said. Silence.

Fortunately, Peter popped out magically from behind some armor. I think we had likely exhausted our conversational possibilities with his (third) wife.

"What a fine pair you make," he said in his trademark deadpan. He was staring at Cherry's breasts lasciviously. He winked at me. Definitely not a blink. Cherry blushed, which is a sign of complete panic for an ex-stripper.

"Why don't you go make yourself at home with Daria, Cherry. Giles and I have some things to discuss mano a mano. We'll see you by the pool." God, I felt for Cherry, but there really wasn't anything to say. We'd been invited for swimming and a casual dinner. So we had brought a bag with changes of clothes. We hadn't been warned to bring a translator though.

He led me up various sets of stairs, and along various

corridors. I wow-ed and ahh-ed obsequiously. He seemed pleased. "Not a bad little crib, hey," he purred.

The journey seemed purely for show, as we sat down in a library having already passed at least two others (some doors were closed, perhaps to give the imagination free rein).

"I haven't just invited you here for fun and games," he began. I started to sweat. He pressed a button on the coffee table between us. Metal screens emerged from everywhere shutting off the windows and doors. Bright lights dazzled from seemingly nowhere. Some kind of gas was being can-nistered in through floor vents. Oxygen, I hoped. That's as much as I could register, though no doubt there was more.

"Relax, Giles," he advised emphatically. No fucking way could I relax. "This is one of my safe rooms. Hermetically sealed, and resistant to all known methods of eavesdropping. It's just safer to talk this way." I relaxed a little. My sphinc-ter unpuckered.

"What do you want to talk about?" I asked as innocently as I could.

"Egon and Zyxview, idiot. What did you think I wanted to talk about? Your wife's favorite position?" I had the impres-sion that that was exactly what he wanted to talk about. But I ignored his Freudian quip by engaging with his professed topic of inquiry.

"What about Egon?…I hardly know him."

"Bullshit, Jill. We hired you because you know him."

"Look, Peter," I said, buckling instantaneously under interrogation. "I don't know him very well. I don't know what gave you the impression I did. I know the stock."

"Why did you get into his limo and drive around with him for well over an hour in San Francisco then? There's no need to pretend here, Giles. We're safe."

"How do you know about San Francisco?" I asked. My sphincter had repuckered.

"I have my sources, Giles. Perhaps you didn't notice the car following you, driven by my spy who was at the dinner in a wheelchair?"

Charlton. It suddenly all made sense. I didn't bother asking about why he was disguised as a cripple. Peter must have overestimated me again.

"I didn't notice," I said truthfully. "I couldn't see out of the limo. But why were you following me?"

"I wasn't, you moron. I was following Egon."

I cursed my stupidity. "But why were you following Egon?"

By the look on his face, I wasn't making it any better on myself.

"Okay, I'm clearly going to have to reduce this to first grade level for you, Giles. I run fund. Fund invests in Zyxview. Zyxview run by Egon. Egon important man. I spy on Egon. I find out where he goes, what he does."

"Is that even legal?"

"Of course it is. I would never knowingly break the law." Another wink that could have been a blink. Either way, it was clearly a lie.

"Then why are we in an impervious safe room?" It seemed like an appropriate, if perhaps impertinent, question.

"Very funny. Back to my question. Why were you driving around with him in his limo?"

"I was just trying to get to know him better, find out a little about what makes him tick."

"And did you?"

"Yes."

"And what did you find out."

"Not a lot." I wasn't sure how much I needed to reveal, even in a safe space.

"That he's a self-hating bisexual?"

"How did you know?"

"He spends a lot of time in and out of bars and apartments in the Castro. Let's just put it that way," Peter said with a smirk.

"Is that relevant?" I asked genuinely.

"Not particularly, but maybe," he replied enigmatically. "What else did you learn? Did he tell you anything he shouldn't have?"

"I don't think so," I replied. "We talked a little about Zyxview. He said they are working on some big things. Nothing that people don't already know."

"But he didn't tell you anything tangible? How the quarter is going? What their products are? When they are launching? What their next press release is going to be?"

"No, of course not. I would never put you in that kind of a quandary." I hoped he could see things from my point of view. I hoped wrong.

"Disappointing, Jill. I was hoping for a lot more than that. Those are the kinds of things I need you to know. You see, I may never knowingly break the law, but you should always break it knowingly." The need for the safe room was more apparent.

"But doesn't that mean you would also be breaking it?"

"Jesus, Jill, of course not. I'm never going to ask you to tell me anything you shouldn't, unless we are in here, which is not likely to happen again. I need you to tell me you know nothing in particular, but have the highest conviction in everything not in particular."

"That's what I just told you," I replied, beginning to see a way out.

"So you are saying that you learned nothing material despite being with him for over an hour? That you have increased conviction in our Zyxview position despite the fact that you had no clue the chief engineering officer was about to resign? I'm trusting that you actually know a lot more than that, and are just smart enough not to tell me, even in this safe space. I'm okay with that, as it's good to get into good habits, but I'm making a big bet that you're lying to me."

"I never lie unknowingly. And I know nothing." My ignorance and ineptitude were again proving my *deus ex machina*. I winked.

"People who blink are usually lying, which is a good thing right now."

"It was actually a wink, though it was communicating the same thing as a blink in this specific situation."

"Don't ever wink at me. Just tell me you have the highest conviction in our Zyxview position and you know everything you shouldn't."

"I have the very highest conviction in our Zyxview position," I answered with an obedient and knowing lie. At least I'd been honest.

"Awesome, Giles. I can see that you are exactly the right person for this job. Well done for getting so close with Egon. I was worried for a bit, I'll be honest. You're setting up for a great career at the fund. I'll make you richer than you can possibly imagine. Meanwhile, as part of my family, I expect you to share everything with me, and I'll share everything with you."

That sounded nice, I'll admit it. Even a minuscule share in Peter's hoards would be more money than most would see in a lifetime of hard work. And I had, by sheer luck and innuendo, managed to get away with having broken no laws, for now. Peter pressed the button again, and we were back in an eighteenth-century library.

"Come on, buddy. Let's go party. I didn't hire you just for your brains."

I didn't want to be his buddy and I didn't want to party with him (whatever that meant). But going with the flow seemed my best option as usual.

BIG AND BUOYANT

"WELL, IF IT isn't Hizzoner," Peter exclaimed, jumping up from his lounger and slapping someone heartily on the back. I'd been lying face down on mine, hoping time would pass more quickly than it was. I reluctantly raised my head.

There is only one thing more bizarre than seeing a socialist mayor at a billionaire's castle. And that's seeing him in his swimsuit. But I couldn't deny reality. There was Bill Smith, champion of the people, all three hundred pounds of him, accompanied by his extremely young-looking third wife, all one hundred pounds of her.

"Who are you?" asked Peter's teenage son Vlad, removing his AirPods for the first time.

"Mayor of New York, son, at your disposal," replied Bill smarmily, proffering a hand. Peter and he shared a hearty laugh.

"Oh, I thought you were famous or something," said Vlad, without so much as moving from the ledge of the pool. There was no handshake. Vlad went back to staring at his phone.

"Don't mind him," said Peter, shaking his head. "I blame his mother for his upbringing." I blamed the Internet. He had that same vacant stare as all teenagers do nowadays. Excessive social media, and in his case, I had zero doubt, porn.

"Bill and Brandy, let me introduce you to Cherry, and her husband, Giles."

Cherry retied the back of her bikini and rolled over like a puppy. "Nice to meet you, Mr. Mayor," she said with a smile. Unlike me, she was clearly feeling much more relaxed. He offered her a hand and she shook it. Feeling obliged I stood up and did the same.

"Nice to see such a beautiful pair." He was also staring at Cherry's breasts. I said they were a work of art. But come on, what is wrong with men? I blame Darwin.

Brandy emerged meekly from behind one of Bill's rolls, and went on her tiptoes to plant a kiss on Cherry's cheek. I politely stooped to peck at her from arm's length.

Formalities over, Bill and Brandy jumped straight into the pool and started paddling (she vigorously, he languidly, supported by his natural floating device).

"Daria will be down shortly, I'm sure," announced Peter. "Thompson—can you go check on her?" he barked to one of the four strapping young men standing at attention by the corners of the Olympic pool, like line judges at a tennis match. I suspected Thompson had checked on her more than once. Or perhaps that was just my filthy mind. Men.

No sooner had Thompson started to move than the bronze double doors to the castle opened, and out came Daria, breast-first. Even I stared this time. She was wearing nothing but a thong and a smile. It wasn't a welcome sight, unless you happen to be an aspiring plastic surgeon. I will spare you the details. Suffice to say she left little to the imagination, unfortunately.

"Jesus, Mum," said Vlad. "Do you always have to go topless by the pool? It's disgusting." He got up and marched off into the house, to watch MILFs in privacy, no doubt.

"You Americans," said Daria, joining the group, "zo prudent. You make ze porn all ze time but no want to see any bosom in the sunshine." She had a point. After all, Cherry and Brandy were barely wearing more than she was. She jumped into the pool, paddling synchronously alongside Bill thanks to her *unnatural* floating devices.

"I'm not prudish," said Cherry, sportingly. She was right of course. But in retrospect I wish she hadn't seen the need to prove it by removing all her remaining covering and gleefully jumping in alongside the floaters. At least Brandy and Daria had the decency to remove the rest of their bikinis in sympathy.

Sometimes I wish I hadn't married a stripper. Rarely though.

XANAXDU

EVERYONE EXCEPT CHERRY looked much better fully clothed and in dim lighting, I observed, as we sat down for dinner.

Vlad's date had joined us, a perky teen called Sam, who predictably spent most of her time taking selfies. She and Cherry had a great time together at the far end of the table, giggling and pointing at each other's phones. In the middle of the table, Vlad, Daria, and Brandy said very little to each other during the feast, as far as I could tell. They focused on the food and drink, I suppose, which was reasonable given that each of the eight courses, served by attractive young ladies in short black dresses, would probably have earned a Michelin star in its own right. I wouldn't have expected less.

If I give you the impression that the socialization was somewhat siloed, it's intentional. You see, the "smallest dining room," as Peter so modestly referred to it, was about the size of my apartment, bedecked in tapestries and lit by huge candle chandeliers. The rectangular dining table would easily have sat twenty; so from our end of the table, which Peter headed, with me on his right and Bill on his left, a shout was required to attract the attention of those in the middle, let alone Cherry and Sam at the opposite end. It was an atavistic seating plan, but I guess Peter knew what he was doing, as we gentlemen clearly had important things to discuss.

"What's the word on the street, Bill?" asked Peter, sitting back to create room for the second dessert no doubt.

"Pre-revolutionary, Peter," said Bill in his familiar stentorian tone. "The masses are sick and tired of the wealthy making the rules and then breaking them. They want social justice…or any kind of justice. They are saddled with debt, sick at the system, and saddened by the world. Apart from that, everything's great."

Peter burst out laughing, almost ejecting his Petrus '82. I would have thought he should be trembling. I was wrong. "Then give them more of what they want."

"What's that?" I asked, trying to get in on things lest I embarrass Peter.

"Stuff," said Bill emphatically. "They want stuff. Not just any stuff. Good stuff. They are Americans after all."

"Bread and circuses," chimed in Peter.

"*Panem et circenses*?" I offered, sensing an opportunity to impress.

"Panim et circuses, exactly," answered Bill, knowingly. "I suspected you only hired the brightest and the worst, Peter." He grinned. "We need to give them more stuff, Giles, to keep them happy."

"Or another *cause célèbre* to distract them from the real problems," suggested Peter. "Like anti-gun campaigns, climate change rallies, LGBTQ rights, or something."

"I've already done that, Peter," answered Bill with a sigh. "That was my first term."

"But don't they understand you are only mayor of New York, not president?" Peter continued. "You can't change crony capitalism by yourself."

I considered mentioning the incongruity of this statement with our setting, but thought better of it.

"Correct. In fact, I can't change *anything*."

"Nothing. But neither can the president," said Peter with a smile.

"Congress?" I asked instinctually.

"Them neither." Bill chuckled. "After all, you guys own them too, don't you, Peter?"

"Just a working majority, Bill, of both parties."

"The judiciary?" I knew the answer before I finished the question.

"Nope. More stuff. That's the only option." Bill smiled paternally. "Which is why I'm about to launch a major campaign to encourage New York's wealthy to give to a charity which will guarantee a free iPhone for every New Yorker—man, woman, and child—so they can get ahead in this increasingly technological world."

"Tax deductible?" asked Peter.

"Of course."

"Count me in."

"Very kind of you, Peter. That's what the people want, so that's what they will get from me. I am the champion of the people after all." Bill laughed. "But how do we pitch it? Perhaps we should ask your expert analyst here. He seems to be married to a girl that knows a thing or two about social media."

He nodded toward the far end of the table, where Sam and Cherry were giggling about something on her iPhone. He was right. Like all politicians he knew the pulse of his electorate.

"Giles?" asked Peter. "You are my technology expert; how would you couch it?"

"Well, I think the key thing," I said after reflecting, "is to emphasize the educational nature of the iPhone. You aren't going to be giving them a phone; you're going to be giving them access to endless opportunities. The chance to get ahead. Equality of opportunity. The American dream. The modern-day abacus and encyclopedia rolled into one." I felt dirty but chuffed at my populist tripe.

"Holy smokes, Peter," bellowed Bill. "The brightest and the worst. He's nailed it. Can you spare him for my next campaign?"

"Absolutely not," said Peter proudly. "I need him to earn me the money to pay for your next campaign, and the non-deductible part of all those iPhones."

They both burst out laughing, like two comic book criminals. I hated politicians almost as much as I hated hedge fund managers, myself included.

"Darrrlinggg," purred Daria from the middle of the table. "Do you think it is time to take them downstairs?"

"Why not? I'm definitely in the mood," exclaimed Peter enthusiastically.

∽

What ensued was without a shadow of doubt the most bizarre incident in my life. And I've had many. But even Lord Quentin Allthorpe and the piglet at the Bullingdon had nothing on this (and I can't even tell you what that was about for fear of prosecution).

We were all led down a monastic circular stairway (Bill had to squeeze a little harder than the rest) that emerged from a trompe l'oeil panel in the smallest dining room, to what could only be described as a dungeon-cum-nightclub, replete with sumptuous chaise lounges, tables full of champagne and liquor, and assorted torture devices hanging from the walls as decoration (I hoped, but doubted).

I immediately went and sat down next to Cherry. "This is weird. I think we should get out of here."

"So weird." She grimaced, pretending to smile. "This feels like the set of *Princess Diaries, The King's Revenge*. Without the cameramen, fluffers, or safe words. I should have known things were going to get crazy when Daria showed me her sex toys earlier."

"She did? Why didn't you tell me?"

"I didn't think much of it. All my girlfriends have sex toys, though perhaps not quite as crazy looking. I thought she was just trying to bond."

"That's what I'm worried about."

"Sweetie, what should we do? I love a good orgy, but not with these freaks. And Sam is like only sixteen. Ugh."

I was cursing myself. How could I have been so naïve to think that Peter's only perversion was mammon? The mayor's antics were well-known. But at a business event? Even my cynicism hadn't envisaged this Tartarus.

Our conversation was drowned out by the incipient beat. As Peter and Daria popped the champagne, the gate to an alcove on the far side of the room opened. I should have known what was coming, but I was still gobsmacked. It was Thompson and his pool boys, led on leashes by the dinner's waitresses, all wearing little save chains and straps. I looked around. No one but Cherry and I seemed the slightest bit concerned. Vlad apparently only took issue to parental sexuality around the pool.

I had seen enough for the day, and more than enough for a lifetime. I grabbed Cherry and walked over to Peter. He got the wrong impression.

"Now we're talking, Giles," he screamed over the beat, grabbing hold of Cherry's ass and beginning to grind.

"We have to get back to the city," I screamed in turn, separating them forcibly.

"Why?" asked Peter, as angry as a wild animal torn from its prey. "Remember, we are a family. We share. What is yours is mine. Some of what is mine could be yours, perhaps."

"I'm sorry, Peter. She's pregnant. Sorry. Perhaps after the baby comes." And with that I yanked her toward the stairway.

"I'm counting on that, Giles," yelled Peter after us. "Otherwise, all bets are off."

I kept going and pushed her up the first steps, before turning to take one last glance back. I should have learned from Orpheus.

The male acolytes were being whipped in time to the beat by their female counterparts, who were completely naked now apart from their dog collars. I hate to say it but not all of me found it as repugnant as I should have. Peter had a nose for talent, me excepted. There was no such ambivalence, let me assure you, at the sight of Bill being frisked under his bottom roll of fat by Brandy, or Vlad unzipping his fly to show Sam his Impaler. Peter gave me a thumbs-up. I gave him one back, and ran.

᪥

Cherry and I managed to retrace our many steps and emerge into a moonlit sky. We clambered back around the cove in silence, and called our Lyft from the one spot we knew it could find.

"It's like fifteen minutes away, honey," Cherry told me when she'd finished tapping away.

"I can wait," I sighed, exhausted.

We sat on a rock and stared out over the sound.

"That was so weird," she said again. Coming from her that meant something.

"I know," I replied laconically.

"You know what's weirder?" she continued after a minute or so lost in thought.

"Nothing," I said emphatically.

"I'm really horny," she said sheepishly. "…For you," she added bashfully.

"You're right, that's weirder," I said, smiling genuinely for the first time since we'd arrived. "But so am I," I confessed. We both laughed, and then made love passionately on top of that rock.

Our missionary mating seemed so pedestrian compared to what was going on nearby that I almost forgot to pull up my pants when the lights of our ride approached. We cuddled up on the backseat and got lost in our thoughts.

"You know what? I need a Xanax," said Cherry after a minute, popping open her purse.

I popped two and fell fast asleep. All is for the best, when on benzos.

AVE IMPERATOR, MORITURUS TE SALUTO

THE SECOND ANNOUNCEMENT was no better than the first. In fact, being the second resignation in so many weeks, it was considerably worse. This time there was no buying at the open. From Peter, or anyone.

It wasn't as if people didn't know who the CFO was. That was supposed to have helped (wasn't it?), as was the fact that he clearly did nothing. But as Peter explained to me in between profanities, the only person those maxims don't apply to is the CFO.

The stock opened down 5 percent and closed down 20 percent. The chart was starting to look considerably less "up and to the right." I adjusted my price target down by 20 percent, thereby keeping it exactly 50 percent above the closing price. Now wasn't the time for vacillation.

"What the fuck?" demanded Peter, calling me down again at the end of the trading day. I couldn't tell whether he was more infuriated at my failure to nail the stock, or his to nail my wife the previous weekend. Perhaps both. Whatever the root of his fury, it sent me into paroxysms of panic. "Why would you take your price target down twenty percent because the stock's down twenty percent?"

"Because I always take it up by twenty percent if the stock is up twenty percent." The logic seemed flawless.

"Listen, bozo, this isn't the sell side. You actually have to be able to explain the movement of your price target with fundamentals, not fabricate the price target from the price. If the fundamentals don't change then neither does your price target."

"But isn't price the most important fundamental for a company without fundamentals?"

I wasn't going to let him win so easily. He was questioning my entire analytical approach, indeed the lynchpin of Wall Street research: the goal-seek function. Without that, the wheels would fall off the entire market.

I should have shut up.

"Who says they don't have fundamentals?" he asked, swiveling around to face me straight on. There was no winking or blinking.

"Fair point," I answered pathetically. I felt like Perseus confronting Medusa. So I returned his gaze via one of the mirrors next to his desk. If I'd been allowed, I would have gladly relieved him of his head. Unfortunately, it looked more likely he'd relieve me of mine.

"Look me in the eye and answer my question," he barked.

I looked him in the eye and blinked, petrified.

"Never wink at me again," he yelled, picking up a calculator and throwing it at my head. I dodged. I didn't dare turn but heard a scream from someone behind me.

"I didn't, I just blinked," I whimpered. I'll be honest; I was close to tears. Perhaps I should have pled with Cherry to give him a BJ. It wouldn't have taken long, I'm sure.

"They have fundamentals, don't they?" he repeated, enjoying himself. Ironically, he would have been great in the

Gestapo, I couldn't help think. "That's a fucking question. Answer it."

"Yes, they do."

"And what are they?"

"That they have no fundamentals."

"Exactly. So I never want to hear you spouting that shit again."

"Absolutely." I would have said "Jawohl" if I'd been in his dungeon. But this was no cosplay. This was real life. There was no safe word. I was being psychologically abused in public for all to see (via the mirrors, of course). And I could hear from the complete silence that everyone was loving it, like dirty old men at a cheap peep show. Peter's private and business worlds were, indeed, perfect reflections of each other.

"So what is your new price target?"

"The same as my old price target?"

"Why?"

"Because the fundamentals haven't changed."

"Bullshit. The CFO resigned."

"He wants to spend more time with his family. That's not a bad thing, surely?"

This time his projectile was an iPhone. It hit me hard in the ear. I squealed like a stuck pig. I couldn't help but think about Daria and Thompson.

"Of course it's a bad thing, Jill. Who wants to do that?" I heard some laughter. He was toying with me for the amphitheater. "Besides, it's not good for the company either."

I decided to play dead and said nothing. I just bled in silence, a novice gladiator at Peter's imperial games.

"So if their fundamental value is that they don't have fundamentals, does the CFO's resignation matter?" he asked violently.

"I don't know," I whined through tears.

"No!" the office bayed in unison.

"See, Giles, they get it, and you don't. You don't get anything, as you proved this weekend." The flashback only made things worse.

In fact, I *had* got it for once. The office had merely repeated what I'd suggested earlier, but I realized that fairness wasn't the point of this exercise in humiliation. The point was that it had no point.

"So what should we do?" he inquired loudly.

"Sell?" I had a 50-50 chance.

"Buy more," everyone yelled in unison. I could hear high-fiving at close proximity.

"And that's exactly what I'm going to do, Jillian, at the open tomorrow. You better hope this thing goes back up or you're dead to me. Now, get the fuck out of here," howled Peter triumphantly, and turned back to his screen. "And get yourself stitched up. I can't stand blood on the carpet." I consoled myself that this clearly wasn't the first time he'd injured an employee.

I'd be lying if I said I was merely wounded physically. *That* only required a quick visit to the ER and two crooked stitches. Mentally, I was undone. And he knew it. Victory. Even Cherry's cheery embrace failed to make it better. I needed Mum, but she was gone.

He bought more at the open the next day. The stock fell another 20 percent. Merrill had downgraded the stock to "Certain Sell," price target 30 percent below the previous day's close. I couldn't really blame the new analyst, Lucy Ho. After all, she used to work for me, and I would have done the same. I would have had the sense to wait till after Friday's close though. She was let go the next week, I heard later.

I couldn't bear to watch the screen that day, so hid under my desk listening to Wagner (that's what my father listened to *in extremis*, so I knew no better). I did the same on Wednesday when it was down another 10 percent in the wake of multiple further analyst downgrades. Clearly Peter and the rest of the office had got this one wrong. A part of me wanted to point that out. The victory would have been pointlessly Pyrrhic, so I stayed under the desk.

"This is a fucking disaster, buddy," said Holton, who had come to ferret me out. "You better get out of here while you still have use of your legs."

"What do you mean?"

"Exactly what I said. Peter's a dangerous guy when you get on his wrong side, and I'm not just talking iPhone scrapes."

"Seriously?"

"Dead seriously. Let's just put it this way: there have been more than a few people at this firm who have met untimely deaths in mysterious circumstances."

"How?"

"Unlikely car accidents, questionable suicides, undiagnosed heart conditions, to name a few. Hey, one guy even got mauled to death by a stray pit bull in Central Park, in front of his kids. Nice guy too. The only common theme is that they were all in Peter's bad books. Sorry, man, but you need to know."

"Fuck." I was puckered tighter than a clenched fist. "Where should I go?"

"I would get on a plane and go talk to Egon. Find out what's happening without actually finding out what's happening, if you know what I mean."

I did, of course. "But he's not talking to me anymore."

"So make him, Giles. I don't want to say this is life or

death. But I also don't want to say it's not. I've seen one or two worse situations. This is probably more like life or permanent disability right now, though it's not trending in a good direction. You either offer Peter your wife as a sacrificial lamb, or you give him what he needs on Zyxview. Those are your only two choices." He had clearly been told, or worked out, what had happened at Xanadu.

I put my head down and began to crawl to the elevators.

"Try not to worry," he added half-heartedly, walking two paces behind me. "I've seen this happen before. Some people live to tell the tale. A few, anyway."

How encouraging.

∽

On my way home I made my decision. I was going to proffer my cherry to Egon, to get the information I needed to save Cherry's from Peter, and us both from a fate that might be worse than death.

If I had any lingering doubts that Holton was serious, they were quickly dispelled when I realized I was being followed.

ANOTHER HUMMER

"DO YOU THINK that's a good idea, baby?" inquired Cherry when I told her my plans (she still didn't know the full scale of the cataclysm, thank goodness) "...What with your stitches. You may get an infection on the plane."

I pointed out to her that dying of sepsis triggered by necrotizing fasciitis was infinitely preferable to another minute near Peter, which was saying something, as dying of anything terrified me to death. I had to explain the medical terms to her.

"I've never heard you this bad before, honey," she said, while snapping a picture of my ear, for Instagram no doubt. "I think you should quit."

"I will, if I can first escape getting fired."

"Okay, that sounds good," she said, unconvinced. "I'm sorry this turned out like this. It's so, so bad. I feel guilty. Perhaps I should have given him a BJ?"

"No way, you're an ex-stripper and movie star, not a hooker. I would never ask you to do something like that."

"Of course not."

"I wouldn't even think about it."

"I know you wouldn't." I was relieved to discover that she didn't know me as well as I feared. Our marriage depended on it.

It was equally healthy for her not to know that I'd whimpered like a schoolgirl in front of the whole office. She'd married me because I was sarcastic ("funny," as she called it ignorantly). She'd made that clear enough. The scene at POS was a laugh at, not laugh with, situation that would have shaken her more than it shook me. Which is saying a lot. There is nothing as unsexy and unappealing as the destruction of a careful crafted veneer of not giving a shit. Our marriage depended on that too.

"Listen, sweetheart," I said, trying and failing to sound blasé. "Things may be bad, but I don't give a shit. I only care about you, our baby, and the Lord Jesus. This is nothing compared to an afternoon at an English public school."

"You're so funny," she purred, fluffing my hair as I hastily packed. "But you don't have to be brave for me. I can tell you're super stressed. I'm here for you whatever happens." She clearly didn't understand our marriage. "And while you're away, I'm going to work on doubling my number of followers. I'm so close to being a major influencer and getting paid for it. It will really help if you lose your job."

"Thanks for the vote of confidence," I quipped. "And how are you going to do that?"

"With these," she said, cupping her breasts up underneath her tight white T-shirt.

"Of course." I managed a little smile. "The twin peaks of prosperity." I wondered what kind of new followers she was hoping to attract, but didn't care. Who was I to interfere with a woman's right of self-expression? I'm an absolute egalitarian when it comes to breasts. In any case, given the predicament I was in, her boobs, though weighty, were the lightest of my worries.

⤥

I boarded the flight to SFO without a hitch and took my seat between a middle-aged couple who had clearly spent most of their married life vying for supremacy at the dinner table. I had to fly coach given the last-minute plans, and to be honest would probably have flown it anyway given I had lost the firm millions of dollars since I joined (call me old-fashioned).

When I suggested to the blobs that they sit together, leaving the window seat for me (I hoped their layers of fat might efficiently meld together), they harangued me for fifteen minutes about having paid extra to select the aisle and window. They were rather annoyed that anyone had taken the middle seat, in fact. When I lied that I was fine in the middle, they harangued me for fifteen more. I put in my earbuds and pretended to listen to music. For once, I wasn't scared of flying. Death didn't seem so bad if it took those two fuckers with me.

I was desperate to pee when we landed at San Francisco. I hadn't dared ask the lady to let me out during the flight, and it would have required mountaineering skills beyond my nonexistent abilities to have gotten over her without straddling her like a horse. It didn't help that she sprang up as soon as the *fasten seat belt* signs were turned off, sandwiching herself effortlessly in the aisle, and thereby preventing me from making a fast escape. To add insult to urgency, I had to wait for two wheelchairs to be brought on to navigate the enormities off the plane. There was no way that elephantine gazelle needed a wheelchair. I suspected they were professional grief merchants and enjoying themselves immensely. This wasn't their first rodeo.

Why tell you all this? Well, it's important that you realize how close to a full mental breakdown I was by this stage. I even began to question my mother's dying words that all was for the best. And as that had been the maxim of my existence, it was as close to suicide as I got.

I touched my bottom at the urinal, so to speak.

Things turned for the better as my swollen bladder drained. They improved even further when Hertz actually managed to find me the Hummer I had spent half an hour requesting from their Indian call center ("Am I hearing, sir, correctly that you are wanting a Hyundai?"—you get the idea).

Even the fact that the same guy who had been following me in New York was waiting for me as I'd left the restroom didn't take me back to the depths of where I'd been before the urinal. As you know, I'd already deduced brilliantly the previous day (from the fact that it was blatantly obvious) that I was being followed. I'd also quickly had the additional insight that the guy wanted me to know that he was following me. I mean why else would a flabby middle-aged man, with peroxide blond hair and gold-mirrored aviators, walk twenty paces behind me for over a mile, stopping when I stopped, wearing nothing but a Taylor Swift T-shirt and tight jorts? The fact he was still wearing the same outfit the next day, all the way on the West Coast, and still walking twenty paces behind me, only confirmed that this was a warning. Peter was watching and wanted me to know he was watching. I wasn't that concerned, I'd decided. If he'd meant me immediate harm, he'd have already made his move.

What's more, I now had a plan. It was a plan that reflected the depth of my desperation. But it was still a plan, which was better than no plan, though only just. I was going directly to Egon's office. And I would camp out there until I got to talk to him, and barter my body for information. I had a sleeping bag, and bought more vegan, non-GMO, organic snacks at Whole Foods on the way to Zyxview than most Bay Area mums eat in a lifetime (and that's all they eat, I'm told). The guy shadowing me bought a melon, incidentally.

∽

It was dark by the time I reached my destination, an office park whose only relationship to the buzz of Palo Alto was the zip code. Sandwiched between two car dealerships on a barren stretch of road near 101, it looked like the kind of place where people could do absolutely nothing without raising suspicion. Which is of course what it was. It looked like most tech headquarters, to be honest. No signage and no obvious signs of life other than the hum of fifty Teslas sucking electricity from a coal-powered power station located somewhere where tech people don't breathe the air.

I anchored the Hummer in the corner of the lot, next to an Escalade ESV that provided some cover in the ocean of electric vehicles. At least one person hadn't got the memo, it appeared, though I reflected that it might just be a company car that employees could beat with branches whenever global warming got too much for them. It was certainly pretty dirty and very isolated in its corner. It was a pariah, whatever its origin or purpose. I felt a great deal of sympathy for it, as you can tell.

I snuck around the side of the car and squinted at the entry for fifteen minutes. No one went in or out. It was probably too dark to tell, anyway. Nor was there any sign of the Taylor Swift guy. Perhaps he'd just been checking where I was going? I decided that I would have a better chance of success finding Egon in the morning, so I rolled out my sleeping bag and fell asleep. That was as far as my plan went. The rest was in God's hands. If he failed me, Peter would make sure I'd be meeting him soon anyway, so I wouldn't have to wait long to lodge a formal complaint.

HERR GOODENOUGH,
I PRESUME?

I WAS WOKEN at daybreak and gunpoint. This was definitely not part of the plan I didn't have. And if this was God's plan, then he was a real shithead. I apologize for the blasphemy—but have you been woken at gunpoint? If not, then please don't judge.

It appeared my cover had been blown by the Escalade, which must have weighed anchor in the middle of the night (I sleep deep). Four Segways had me cornered, and all four of their uniformed riders had machine guns trained on me. Overkill, undoubtedly, but I wasn't going to point that out.

Thirty minutes later, having successfully avoided been fully overkilled by unlocking the car with my teeth (I had watched enough cop shows to know to keep my hands inside my sleeping bag), I was back in some kind of dungeon. It was a habit I seemed destined to unwillingly acquire.

I had been blindfolded and manhandled into the building by a side door, after professing that I was a friend of Egon's and was merely waiting for him to arrive at work. They had been, quite reasonably, unconvinced. When I'd suggested the blindfold was unnecessary, as I already knew where I was, they had been, quite unreasonably, unconvinced. At least they were consistent. When you are protecting absolutely nothing, it is critical to take all available precautions, it seems.

Having pushed me down a couple of flights of stairs, they had removed my blindfold. They needn't have bothered. It was pitch back. They must have been navigating with night goggles unless they knew this room inside out. Either possibility was equally unlikely and irrelevant. They had handcuffed me to a metal chair and left. Barry, apparently the leader of the unit, needed a cigarette. They had never returned.

Two hours later someone entered and turned on floodlights. It took me at least a minute of wincing and blinking to make out the unmistakable fur vest of Egon Crump.

"We meet again, 007," said Egon, stroking his fur menacingly.

"Hi, Egon," I answered. I should have spent more time preparing for this moment, but had instead been reflecting on the meaning of life in the context of the meaninglessness of everything. I quickly shifted to working on how to offer myself to him. It was going to be hard given the handcuffs, though he'd probably enjoy it even more that way. Fortunately, he spoke again before I'd had a chance to finalize a plan.

"That was quite possibly the worst attempt at subterfuge I've ever encountered," he snapped, kicking off his flip-flops and putting his feet up on the table between us. I thought momentarily about recommending Tinactin but sensibly focused on more pressing issues.

"That's because it wasn't subterfuge," I countered, deciding for the time being there was no rush on prostration. "I just arrived at SFO late and decided to wait out in the car park for our meeting."

"What meeting?" he asked, intrigued.

"This one." If he recognized the circular reference, he didn't let on.

"Why did you try to conceal yourself behind my girlfriend's Escalade then? There was plenty of parking up front."

"I didn't want to take up an EV charging space. Doing my bit for the planet."

"You could have parked in a disabled spot," he ventured, hoping to trap me.

"I didn't know disabled spots don't have EV ports," I responded truthfully.

"Bullshit. Everyone knows that. We considered it, but were concerned the losers might try to jerry-rig them to charge their wheelchairs. Also, most disabled people are old and can't afford Teslas."

"What about Bolts?" I had decided that going with the flow might be my best option for now, till I had some idea of where this was headed.

"I hadn't thought about that," he admitted. "I'll look into it again."

"That's a good idea. Your disabled employees will thank you."

"I don't have any disabled employees."

"Why not?"

"No place for them to charge their cars."

This was going nowhere fast. I shut up and waited for his next move.

"So if this wasn't subterfuge, Giles, then why didn't you just request the meeting we're now having?"

"Because you told me you never wanted to hear from me again."

"You could have asked your EA to speak to mine."

"I assumed, Egon, that you had a more general embargo on me in mind."

"I did."

"Then having my EA talk to your EA wouldn't have worked."

"You're dead right, douche. I would never have let her organize a meeting with a low-down, dirty spy like you who took advantage of my fucking good manners to probe me for company secrets. And in the back of my limo too. That place is like my home. In fact, some nights it is my home."

"But you're the one who pulled me into it." I wasn't sure which objection to raise first.

"That doesn't give you the right to spy."

"I'm not a spy. I'm a hedge fund manager. I can't spy for shit. This morning should tell you that."

"So you *were* trying to spy here then, asswipe?"

"I didn't say that. I said that *if* I had been a spy, you would have known that I wasn't a spy by the fact that I can't spy for shit. And any case what has that got to do with your limo in San Francisco? I hadn't even been here yet."

"Once a spy always a spy," he continued, impressed with his anachronistic logic.

"Does that apply retroactively too?"

"You fucking bet it does."

"But I wasn't spying in the limo, I was just asking probing questions."

"They weren't probing. In fact, if I remember correctly probing was exactly what you weren't willing to do or receive."

My sphincter puckered. It has that tendency in moments like these, as you know. This incident was more apropos than most. I thrashed around to get to the bottom of things, as it were. "Exactly, I wasn't even probing. Just asking dumb questions."

"Actually, I seem to remember your insight being genius, though I admit I may have had a little too much on board to remember jack shit."

"So why did you think I was spying?"

"Because Bill told me you were."

"Who's Bill?" I couldn't help thinking of Big Bill Smith, mayor of New York. I had a flashback to my most recent stay in a dungeon, and felt nauseous.

"Bill my fixer, Bill my detective, Bill my driver." Now I remembered Bill.

"Bill was spying on me?"

"Nope."

"Then why did he think I was spying on you?"

"Because someone was spying on him, dickweed."

"Me?"

"Were you?"

"No."

"Then who?"

"You tell *me*!" I screamed. "Or let me go." I'd had enough of this Punch and Judy Show.

"I'll tell you then. Your partner in the wheelchair." Egon played his trump card and took the trick. Of course, Charlton. My brain raced furiously to recalibrate.

"Work your way out of that one, traitor," he said with a grin.

"You've made a mistake," I mumbled at last.

"Go on."

"You see, it is true that Charlton works for Peter. And it's true that I work for Peter. But it's not true that I knew Charlton worked for Peter."

"Who's Charlton?"

"The guy in the wheelchair."

"You're lying again. His name is Bertram Barnacle and he used to work for MI6."

"That can't be his name."

"Yes it is. Dawn (aka Bill) knew him from her CIA days. He must be the worst spy the Brits ever created. He didn't even recognize her, but then her disguise as Bill is perfect, so I don't blame him. You've seen him more recently as a middle-aged pedo."

"Bertram's a pedophile?"

"I don't know, peanut. But as he's been following you around wearing a Taylor Swift T-shirt and jorts, I assume that's the look he's going for. Don't worry, we picked him up yesterday outside Whole Foods. He's in our custody, and we're going to find out what you two have been up to when he finally talks. He was packing some serious heat by the way."

Damn, if Bertram was that obvious as Charlton, perhaps he *hadn't* in fact wanted me to know he'd been following me as a pedo, which meant perhaps he had just been waiting for the right time to knock me off. He was packing heat somewhere. Where, I hesitated to think about. More importantly, had I just avoided assassination? Fuck. Had Egon saved me? And how could Bertram be so useless when he'd managed to look completely different from Charlton as the pedo? As these thoughts raced through my head, Egon continued.

"So, Jill, you might as well tell me the truth. We know you and Bertram are working together right now spying on me. And we know you were back in San Francisco that night too."

"Back when Dawn was disguised as Bill, and Bertram as Charlton?" I asked in wonder. "No one can possibly be called Bertram Barnacle, by the way. You've been played."

"That's irrelevant," he went on. "The point is there is no Charlton, or pedo, only Bertram, and yes, Dawn was at the time disguised as Bill, idiot," chided Egon.

I finally saw the mistake.

"You are right, Egon, there isn't a Charlton."

"No, there isn't," he interrupted. "And you are a liar and a spy."

"I'm neither, and Charlton, I mean Bertram, was never really Charlton. That's just what I called him."

"So you admit you did know him? You're not doing yourself any favors here, sunshine."

"For fuck's sake, Egon, I didn't know him. I just called him Charlton because he spoke like Charlton Heston."

"No, he doesn't. I just spoke to him. That's how we know he works for Peter. He sounds like William H. Macy."

"But he *did*—remember the dinner? He was in disguise. His computer voice sounded like Charlton Heston."

"No, it didn't. It sounded like James Earl Jones."

"More like Charlton in *Ben Hur*."

"Perhaps," Egon conceded gallantly. "So what?"

"Well, that's why I called him Charlton. I didn't know him. I thought he was just another investor."

"No investor is smart enough to put that disguise together. They're generally not smart enough to tell the difference between a semiconductor and a superconductor."

"I'm an investor and I have no idea about the difference."

"Exactly."

"Thanks, Egon. But the more important point is that I didn't *know* he was disguised, then or now. Nor did you, remember?"

"True. Though I had my suspicions. My mother died

hooked up to one of those, and her computer never sounded like Charlton Heston."

"So did mine, Egon, if you remember, and hers sounded just like Mr. Heston."

"I think you'll find it was probably more like James Earl Jones."

"As Darth Vader?" I asked. He nodded. "No way," I objected. "Darth's pitch is at least an octave lower than Ben's, and his timbre completely different."

"Who's Ben? What the fuck are you talking about?" He was now clearly more confused than I was. I'd turned the tables, but wasn't out of jail yet.

"Okay, let me summarize," I said calmly, "and please hear me out. It is really pretty simple if you follow the logic. I am at this meeting here that we didn't arrange, not because I'm a spy but because I came to see you. I came to see you to find out what happened that made you tell me never to see you again. Now I know. You think I'm a spy because you think I was spying last night along with Bertram (aka Pedo), based on the assumption that a spy is always a spy. Hence I must be a spy because Bertram (aka Charlton as Ben, or James as Darth, depending on whose opinion you trust) works for the same guy as I do, Peter, so I must have been spying in concert with him that night in San Francisco, and ready to do the same here. But I'm telling you that Dawn (aka Bill) was wrong to conclude that I know Bertram. In fact, I only found out about Bertram from Peter when he told me Bertram was spying on you last weekend at the orgy."

"How do you know about my orgy if you aren't a fucking spy?" asked Egon, stunned.

"No, not *your* orgy." I corrected my malapropism

immediately. I wasn't surprised by the confusion. "*Peter's* orgy, which wasn't actually an orgy. Well, it was, but we didn't participate."

"Like Bill Clinton and the joint?" asked Egon. "Come on, I know you were right in the thick of it, sexy. You can tell me. It's okay to get a kick out of group sex. How many people were there? Boys or girls? Was it bi or straight?"

He was getting excited and it wasn't helping us.

"Egon, please, it doesn't matter if I was participating or not."

"It matters to me, Jill."

"I'll tell you about it later. The important thing is that I'm not a spy because Peter only told me about Bertram at *Peter's* orgy last weekend. So when I was in the limo with you, I had no idea Bertram was spying on you. Everything I said in there was genuine. And I had no idea that the pedo following me around was the same guy (aka Bertram) that Peter sent to spy on you in the wheelchair. I assumed he was just some guy hired to intimidate me because I refused to let my wife sleep with Peter at his orgy. Think about it, if we were working together, then why was he following me?"

I slumped in the chair. That wasn't easy to effect as it was metal, and I was still attached to it by the wrists.

After a minute of silence that seemed like an hour, the judge and jury rose. "I knew it all along," said Egon triumphantly, unlocking my handcuffs with a key he took out of the center of his leather pants. "I told Dawn you were legit. She wasn't sure. Which is why we took extra precautions this morning. I'm sorry, man. Sorry for everything. It all makes sense now. Come on, let's go chat upstairs. We'll have to check with what's left of Bertram, of course, but I believe you."

My sphincter unpuckered proudly, having just set a new personal best.

As he opened the door, Egon turned and looked at me in the eye. "I just have one more question before we go up."

"Sure, anything," I stated confidently. I knew I wasn't a spy (at least not in that sense) and was prepared for any new line of inquiry.

"Were there trannies at Peter's orgy too?"

OMNIA VINCIT AMOR

AFTER HAVING HIS remaining kneecap broken, apparently Bertram confirmed my story, so I was home and dry in that respect at least. As an aside, I've never found out what happened to him. To be frank, I couldn't care less. He could well have been about to kill me. I had my suspicions he'd received an equivalent payback.

Egon and I spent an hour together in his office once I'd been cleared. It was the most normal hour I've spent with him, despite it being a decidedly un-normal office. To be fair, it would have been a pretty un-normal hour too by anyone else's standards. Except maybe Peter's.

Whereas the rest of the building could have been the headquarters of any of the tech companies I hadn't bothered visiting, Egon's office was accessed through a pair of swinging saloon doors. Inside was a replica of a Wild West bar, straight out of a John Wayne movie. Literally. He'd bought it at auction, he told me proudly.

"This saloon tells you more about me than any bio, Jill. It's a subtle riff on my life."

"I wouldn't say it's subtle."

"Man, I love you. You just say it like it is. No one has the balls to tell me the truth."

"Thanks."

"But you are completely fucking wrong. It's very subtle. Tell me what you think it says about me. Let's see how much research you've actually done on me, princess."

I'd read his Wikipedia entry, which was a lot of research for me.

I knew he was born Egon Petrescu in Romania, the only child of a pair of carnies who defected to the west in the '80s while in a traveling circus. They subsequently prospered at Barnum and Bailey, before his mother broke her neck in a freak trapeze accident involving a dwarf. His father settled in LA, where he died of alcoholism a few years later, leaving Egon to be raised by a series of foster families (one of whose last names he adopted). Egon was a math whiz who won a number of scholarships, ending up at MIT, where he rode the first dot-com bubble by launching a website (I forget its name) that was bought by Yahoo in 1999 for cash (and was subsequently written down as worthless). He then went quiet till he founded AppApp in 2007, foreseeing that the iPhone would provide the gas for a new Internet bubble, blown around apps. He sold AppApp shortly thereafter for $500M, before it amounted to much beyond its potential. It was written down as worthless a year later. Meanwhile, he'd founded Zyxview.

As I ran through all this in my mind, I couldn't see the immediate connection to the Wild West, so punted. "I'm not a spy, remember? I don't know much about you."

"I know you're not a spy. Think metaphorically, dude."

"You like whiskey and hookers?"

"That's not metaphorical; that's factual."

"Is it?"

"Factual in concept, d-bag. Not as it pertains to me."

"But I thought you did."

"That's irrelevant. The point is, the place tells you something about my dreams."

"Whiskey and hookers?" I couldn't really get where he was going.

"No, the fucking American Dream, Jill."

"Exactly," I taunted. "Whiskey and hookers."

"Quit it, Groucho. You know what I mean. The American frontier. The place where every man can start afresh, build something for himself, and double his fortune at cards."

"And then be shot dead in the blink of an eye."

"Now you're getting it. The American Dream. Living on the edge, self-reliance, hatred of convention, disrespect for bureaucracy…"

"…and devil take the hindmost."

"Why not? We don't need losers, Giles. Just winners. Who is John Galt? I am, for fuck's sake. Hashtag torpedo-of-truth, hashtag winning."

"Hashtag you bet you are," I said, slapping him on the back. "Hashtag Zyxview."

"Yup, that's it," he affirmed seriously. "That's what Zyxview is. It's one hundred and fifty percent proof winning."

"Doing nothing."

"Pretending to do nothing, while actually doing something, in fact, hypothetically."

"What?"

"You know I can't tell you, or you and the company will be ruined." He was right.

"But then why are people leaving? Obviously, I don't want you tell me anything you can't, but why are people leaving?" If he wouldn't tell me, I was ready to offer him what I knew he still wanted. My hope was either way he'd do it in a way that left me unscathed.

"Well, I don't know. But I could posit that it's because they think we're doing nothing. Only I know we are doing something, because only I am doing it. Alone. Okay, with the help of a small team of engineers, a small team of contract manufacturers, and a small team of computer scientists, but none of them know what they are doing because none of them work at Zyxview, and none of them can see the whole picture. That's why I can tell you."

"You mean Zyxview's first product is not part of Zyxview?"

"Correct. It's part of Zyxview's first spinout. I've separated it completely from Zyxview. It has its own ownership structure and everything. Me. That way I don't have to worry about Zyxview having a product."

"So the guys who are leaving Zyxview are right. They aren't actually doing anything?!" I was back to hedging my tone.

"No, they are wrong, because although *they* may not be doing anything, *we* may doing something."

"The royal we?"

"Precisely, Columbo. And they're too stupid to realize that by hypothetically doing nothing, they are fulfilling their role of hypothetically enabling me to do something. Which is a pity for them as they'd all make a hypothetical fortune if I were to sell Peach to Zyxview."

"Peach," I mused. "What exactly does it do?"

"Well, I probably shouldn't tell you that even if it's not part of Zyxview."

"True," I replied, happy he'd not led me over the line, though I was having trouble being sure where it was given all the permutations and combinations. "So is Zyxview worthless then?"

"No, it's worth a fortune, as I tell investors publicly every day."

"How?"

"Its market cap is still north of twenty billion dollars even following this minor pullback."

"Fifty percent isn't minor," I observed.

"It is, given the upside potential that I'm going to unlock."

"And how are you going to unlock it when Zyxview may in fact not do anything?" I asked, despite feeling I should somehow be able to work it out.

"Because it's changing the world."

"Oh yes, I forgot."

"And because when the timing is right, I might sell it Peach for a fortune, in cash."

"And how would it raise the cash, hypothetically, to buy Peach, whatever that is?"

"The way it always has done. By selling shares in a secondary to fucking morons like you."

"But who's going to buy more shares down fifty percent from the high, with executives departing?" I wondered aloud, knowing Peter wasn't going to, and if Peter wasn't, no one would.

"Wall Street."

"No, they won't."

"Yes, they would."

"No, they wouldn't, Punch. Peter is thinking of selling, I'm sure. The chart isn't up and to the right."

"Correct, Judy. But it will be soon."

"It needs to double to get back to where it was a couple of weeks ago," I pointed out helpfully.

"I can double this baby in minutes."

"How?"

"You really don't know?"

"No."

"I like you, bro, but you can be pretty fucking retarded sometimes."

"Developmentally challenged," I insisted.

"No, retarded," replied Egon with a maniacal stare. "You came up with the genius insight yourself, though I'm now starting to question whether you just hit on it by luck."

"Not me," I lied. "I've never been lucky enough to qualify for unintentional genius."

"Well, it was intentional genius then. You must just be a moron in regular conversation, which is fine by me. Actually, it is one of your most beguiling characteristics. I fucking love it. You're like that picture of Einstein with his tongue out. Pure fucking genius, hiding behind a clown's mask. I just wish you'd also get *your* fucking tongue out more often. And your pant tongue, while I think about it." I wished he hadn't been thinking about it. My sphincter...but I'd do whatever it took, if necessary.

"Well, what was it?" I asked, quickly trying to redirect him.

"What was what?"

"My genius insight?"

"You know I can't tell you that, Giles. Just use that thing inside your brain called memory."

I tried to remember. But all I could remember about that car ride was everything I'd been trying to forget.

Egon shook his head. "Why all this playing dumb? I know you know."

"You do?"

"The announcement."

I remembered "...of an announcement."

Perhaps I was a genius after all. All is for the best.

"You may think that, Jill, but I couldn't comment," he said with a wink. "And one more thing, Jill, I'm in love with you."

As I'd gotten all of what I needed, self-sacrifice was fortunately no longer necessary.

VENUS DE DESHAUN

I FLEW BACK to New York on winds of euphoria and in a first-class seat. Even better, there were three wheelchairs that came on board behind me as I exited the aircraft. Those at the back of economy class were going to be there for a while. The schadenfreude was blissful. In fact, the only downer was that I had rediscovered my fear of flying as a necessary corollary of rediscovering a life worth fearing for. It was a price I was more than willing to pay.

I was even secretly delighted that one of America's tech titans had confessed his true love to me. So what if he was an insane, immature, impulsive sociopath? Weren't they all? So what if I wasn't in the least bit interested in leaving Cherry for a life of dissolute debauchery with another man? So what if he cried in my arms like a baby when I told him, nuzzling my pecs and sucking his thumb? He loved me and that was something, which as you know is more than nothing. His love was so pure that he didn't even try to grab my balls when we embraced to say goodbye. And he didn't even try to change my mind after the first ten times.

I wasn't the only one as giddy as a toddler at the teat of a helium balloon. Cherry had doubled her followers while I'd been away. She'd announced her pregnancy via a photo of herself wearing nothing but body paint and a pout. I was delighted for her, gladly ceding the visuals to the public in exchange for the full 5D version at home.

"You don't think I went too far, do you?" she asked eagerly from the sofa, uncrossing and re-crossing her cervine legs while grazing on a recyclable bag of "puppy chow."

"No way, Jose-phina. You went just far enough. After all, you've gone further in your career."

"I know, sweetie, but no one can find that stuff unless they're porn hounds."

"So that includes at least three-quarters of the men in the world. The rest still don't have broadband."

"But they totally don't know my name unless they hang on till the credits."

"Fair point. No risk of that. And this is definitely more public and less pubic than your prior work. In one snap you've shaved more than just a few minutes off your previous performances."

"You're so funny." She giggled, apparently satisfied at my cavalier attitude. "DeShaun did a helluva job, don't you think?"

"Yes, your body looks as taut as a trampoline. What would Father say? *Tum omnibus una omnis subripuit Veneres*?"

"Ooh, that is so sexy...I mean like when *you* say it." The ensuing pause was as pregnant as she was. "But I meant didn't DeShaun do such a great job on the *body paint*? He's a real artist."

"I didn't realize DeShaun was allowed to work on your body art as well as your abductors," I said flippantly, despite a rising pang of jealousy that I did my best to send swiftly back to its origin. Now wasn't the right time to debate the parameters of our fairly open marriage.

"Do you like my new shade? It's selling like hot cakes," she asked, shifting the subject with a nod toward her iPhone, which I was now scrolling through with renewed interest.

"The one on your lips or your three bull's-eyes?" I asked, switching back to Instagram.

Her breasts had been painted as a pair of pastel targets, with black dots on the nipples. The rainbow over her valley similarly drew the eye down to a black vanishing point. I wondered if she'd allowed DeShaun free rein over the full canvas. I sent the pang back again.

"My lips, silly! I'm calling it Ravishing Red."

"Well, I'm sure that's what @dirtylarry69 must have been thinking about when he wrote "I wanna f*** you, baby grrrlll." I had made the mistake of reading some of the comments from her new followers.

"Perhaps he is talking about his wife?" she asked as she typed laboriously on her laptop. "It seems like he bought two lipsticks from the store, anyway. I sold hundreds today."

"I don't want to know what he's going to do with those," I replied facetiously, unshackling myself from my momentary angst with the strongest cynicism I could muster.

"Stop being totally gross. What's wrong with you?" she half joked.

"I'm a man."

"…a dirty man," she said, hopping up naked and grabbing me greedily. The number of articles of clothing she wore was always inversely proportional to her happiness.

"…a very happy dirty man," I grunted.

"I'm so proud of you for sorting everything out on your trip, dirty man," she purred, looking me deep in the eyes, the exquisite tip of her nose caressing mine. "I was getting worried about you." I melted. It felt better than two Xanax, which is saying something.

"Egon just needed to be taken in hand," I mused enigmatically. There was a time and a place to tell her the whole story. This was neither.

"Well, come take *me* in hand, dirty daddy," she echoed in a whisper.

We spent the rest of the day in bed.

MIRROR, MIRROR ON THE WALL

I WORE MY best poker face entering the office.

"Why are you looking so pleased with yourself?" asked Holton within minutes. "Be careful, boss. Peter's not going to want to spend all day with that smug grin in one of his mirrors."

"I couldn't care less. Peter's going to like me again sooner or later."

"In-ter-es-ting," he said. "Sounds like someone knows something they shouldn't."

"Nope. I know nothing I shouldn't and everything I should. Which is basically nothing in particular."

"All right, Yogi. Congratulations on whatever the 'nothing' is you don't know." He winked, unmistakably. "But just to clarify something: Peter never liked you. Don't know where you got that idea from."

"Oh. I guess he just liked my wife."

"Precisely." His confidence was odd.

"How do you mean?"

"Forget about it for now," he whispered, as nervously as a diabetic at an ice cream parlor. "There are a few things we need to discuss. How about we grab drinks soon?"

"Sure."

He bent over my desk looking for something. There was nothing there of course. He grabbed a pen and paper from the empty desk next to me. "Same place, tonight at 7," he wrote, before folding the paper neatly and putting it in his pocket. I nodded conspiratorially.

"Great, nice job," he suddenly shouted, and punched me on the arm with a thump that left me close to tears. Everyone near me turned to stare enviously. If they'd felt the pain I was feeling, perhaps they would have been more sympathetic. Who was I kidding? They were psychopathic cannibals ready to feast on me given the slightest excuse, and my obvious pain was merely an amuse-bouche to whet their ravenous appetites.

෴

I spent the rest of the day improving my Zyxview valuation model by making sure that it was completely incomprehensible to anyone but me, lest someone ask for it and realize that it was, in fact, just completely useless.

This mostly involved adding extra worksheets with dozens of hidden cells and layers of grouped sub-formulas that in turn drove assumptions, which led to the drivers of the assumptions in the main pro forma financial statements that I had modeled out in excruciating detail thirty-five years out, which in turn flowed into summaries of those statements, which fed a discounted cash flow valuation matrix, comparable multiple valuation matrix, sum-of-the-parts valuation matrix, and liquidation valuation matrix, which in turn led to the valuation summaries that led to the master sheet, which provided the calculations that spat out the base case price target at the center of a pretty yellow table, encased in a very professional solid black border.

That master sheet was the only thing I ever printed out

and showed anyone, and they always nodded sagely, as if staring at the Magna Carta (perhaps because I had it printed in the highest color resolution on very expensive extra-thick presentation paper that I brought in specially for the purpose). But what with the pressure on the stock, I felt one couldn't be too careful. Plus, I had absolutely nothing else to do.

All I had to do was tweak a couple of key inputs hidden deep in some indecipherable subsections of subsections, and as if by magic I could get the base case price target to wherever I thought it should be, currently 200 percent above the current price (if you remember, Peter had commanded me not to move it as the stock went down, and who was I to question such a promulgation?). At eighty-five pages of dense computation that took several minutes to run when a couple of cells changed, the chance of anyone wanting to try to decipher it was as close to zero as the chance of anyone actually reading the whole of *Ulysses*.

In that sense it was, to be frank, a standard sell-side model, designed to lull the buy-side into thinking that an enormous amount of work had been done, which it had—not in illuminating the true fair value of a company, but rather in obfuscating the fact that every recommendation was really determined by where the stock had closed the previous day, and thereby the likelihood that any given recommendation would drive trading commissions, which generated the large fees that paid the stupendous bonuses that everyone was always disappointed by.

The added advantage of doing this unnecessary legwork was that I couldn't possibly be grinning at the same time, given that it required my deepest concentration (and a fair amount of luck) to grow the writhing beast while protecting it from suicidal entropy. Fortunately, I could always revert to a previous version *in extremis* (which provided the same answer, of course).

You see, the bigger it got the more risk there was of it suddenly succumbing to the death throes of the circular reference. When that happens the modeler has about five minutes to operate on the fiend, tracking down a hopefully recent mistake, before even a chess grandmaster would have to accept that the thing is FUBAR. FUBAR was bad, as FUBAR replaced the pretty yellow table of highly implausible valuations with a jungle of #REF!s. And #REF!s meant going back to a previous version and starting the entire process of feeding the animal again. And that took time, time which I didn't have, as I'd already penciled in doing nothing for the rest of the week.

After the hardest day's pointless work in weeks, I successfully alchemized my Frankenstein's monster in time for tea. It did exactly what I told it to, and I was as happy as a dog with two bones. I just prayed it wouldn't take revenge on me someday.

"Giles, come down to my desk now," Peter's voice boomed over the system at the close.

Surprisingly, I wasn't scared of him anymore. I knew I now held the trump cards, and I was more curious than anything. As a sign of my confidence, I even brought a fresh copy of my valuation summary that the printer had nearly died giving birth to a few minutes earlier. It was, of course, the same summary as the last one. But with all those extra sheets and formulae behind it, it felt somehow heavier and more impregnable.

"Please explain to me why you have been grinning idiotically all day," asked Peter without turning from his vast dashboard.

"I haven't, Peter," I replied lazily. "I was grinning when I got in and grimacing for the last several hours." I realized that my concentration face must have given the wrong impression. I didn't blame him. He hadn't seen it before.

"It looked like a grin to me."

"No, Peter, it was a grimace. I always grimace when working hard."

"I've never seen you grimace before," he replied. I'd foolishly hung my own noose.

"I think you have," I blurted, desperately searching for something to cut it down... "Though I admit sometimes my grimace looks like a smirk, which could be mistaken for a grin."

"A fucking smirk?"

"More of a fucking scowl, if I'm honest."

"Listen, Jill. I'm one inch away from causing you permanent brain damage." I didn't doubt him. I just wasn't worried anymore.

"Well, an inch is plenty," I offered reasonably.

And then a strange thing happened. He paused. I'm sure no one had ever talked to him like this. He was discombobulated.

"Look, I'm not a psycho, but I'm pretty pissed. Zyxview is down again today, and down over fifty percent since you joined. I hate losing money, that's all."

"Well, I have several recommendations, Peter. First, stop acting like a psycho if you don't want to be taken for one. Second, have confidence in your analysts. And third, stop caring about money. You've got more than half of the city combined." I laughed out loud and slapped him on the back. I don't know where this sudden rush of bravery came from, but I really didn't care. The office was now humming audibly.

Peter didn't reply. He just turned slowly in his chair. He

looked like a boxer staggering up from a knockout. But he didn't completely give up the fight.

"Fair point, I suppose," he slurred. "But why should I have confidence in you when you've been so completely wrong about Zyxview?"

"Wrong today, right tomorrow, who knows? Life is short, Peter, as your friend Bertram knows. The price is irrelevant. I have conviction." I winked at him.

"Conviction?" he asked. The mention of Bertram had unsettled him visibly, though he showed no inclination to verbally address it.

"Real conviction." I quietly slipped the pretty valuation table in front of him.

"This is the same price target as before," he said, handling it like a holy relic.

"Of course, Peter. Nothing has changed."

"Nothing?"

"Nothing in the fundamentals. And that's what matters."

"Yup, you're dead right there."

"Only my conviction has increased."

"Good," he said quietly, as if to himself. "Then I'll buy some more."

"Why don't you," I suggested. "Don't listen to those idiots on the Street."

"But you were one of them only a few weeks ago," he complained.

"Ah, but that's before I met you, Peter."

"You're damn right it was. Okay, Jill, I was going to fire you or worse. But I'll give you another chance. I'm going to assume your little trip out West was fruitful. I'll buy some more. You'd better hope you're right though," he said, regaining some composure. "Or you're out of here. And good luck finding another job, or another life for that matter."

"Thanks, Peter," I said, and walked back to my desk. The ripple of noise that followed me was somewhere between a cheer and a hiss. Which was about as good as it got at POS.

All is for the best.

HOUSE OF CARDS

I SNUCK INTO the bar incognito at 6:45 p.m.

"Hi there, mister," said the same server we'd had the previous time around. "Nice to see you again. What can I get for you?" I suspected Holton had left her a juicy tip.

"I'll take a dry Manhattan straight up."

"You got it."

Holton arrived at seven sharp. He entered wearing shades below a black baseball cap that he had pulled down to his eyebrows, and was wearing a large black overcoat. He must have been sweating like a sumo wrestler in a sauna. If this was his attempt at disguise on a hot August evening, it was hopeless, as he was both incongruous and recognizable. He should have asked Bertram for some tips. But perhaps Bertram was no more. It certainly seemed like a possibility from Peter's reaction to his name.

"Hey, buddy," he said furtively. "Let's get an alcove." I followed obediently. Everyone in the crowded bar was now watching us.

We settled into an alcove that was only visible to half the room and hunkered down. He peeled off his layers. As expected, he'd been sweating profusely, leaving large patches of moisture around his barrel chest. He looked awful.

"You can't be too careful," he whispered. I nodded or shook my head. I can't remember which. Either would have worked.

"I'll have two of whatever he's having," he said to our server, who had had no difficulty whatsoever in finding where to bring my drink.

"Coming right up," she said inanely. He ogled her perky tail as it swished back to the bar.

Several minutes of small talk later (mainly involving our server), his sweat patches had started to fade, and he seemed ready to dive into the main pool of the conversation.

"Look," he said gravely, "I need to get your thoughts on something. You seem like the kind of guy who can get to the bottom of things quickly." I laughed. I assumed it was a joke.

"It's not funny," he went on. "There's something odd going on with Peter."

"Odder," I suggested unhelpfully.

"Okay, odd-er-er. And it tangentially involves your Zyxview position."

"Interesting," I said genuinely.

"You see, he sold the entire equity position and replaced it with a complicated synthetic derivative position involving a lot of butterflies and collars."

"Hmm…" I hummed, trying to sound both intrigued and informed. I didn't have a clue what he was talking about, of course. Options and the like were way above my pay grade. And as for collars, that only reminded me of one thing.

"Exactly," he continued, seemingly convinced. "Why would he do that?"

"Indeed, why?" I put the ball back in his court.

"Exactly. Why?" I kept quiet. When he realized that was as much as I had to offer, he continued. "Yes, why, that's what

I keep asking myself. On the one hand, it means that if we get to your price target, he makes a lot more money, I think, but if we don't, and soon, we lose everything."

"Everything?"

"Yup, everything. And that's not like Peter. I mean he clearly has a ton of conviction now in your conviction. But this was all done before today, when he had no conviction in your lack of conviction."

"I had lots of conviction," I said defensively.

"I know, but he had no conviction in your lots of conviction. It's like he knew he was going to suddenly have a lot of conviction in your conviction, or…" He paused and looked around. "Or, he's trying to free up capital for something else." I knew just enough to understand that options meant less money down and more risk of total loss. That's why I hadn't bothered to learn more. It sounded like gambling. And I was terrible at poker.

"Hmm…" I repeated, satisfied in the outcome of my first hum.

"In and of itself, I wouldn't be concerned, dude. Peter's not the least aggressive person I know, and he always likes to have a big base of capital in case some brilliant new idea comes along. But he could do that by taking on more leverage."

"Leverage…" I nodded wisely. I'd exhausted the value of humming.

"So, Giles, why does he see the need to free up more capital when he could just use leverage?"

"Indeed, why?" I wasn't going to change tack now.

"What's particularly concerning is that we've had some pretty big redemptions. One of Peter's lieutenants left six months ago to start up a new fund and has been winning over some of our investors by promising to do exactly what Peter does for less."

"That makes sense."

"I guess so. And they've got a new COO who was better than me at lacrosse and tells better schoolgirl stories, apparently. Peter is furious at me. It's not fun."

"Ouch," I said. I was about to point out that I knew how he felt, as I was finding it hard to lift my martini glass to my lips without triggering a sharp pain in my arm where he had punched me. But I didn't want to disrupt the flow.

"Anyway, and here's the real catch. When I went to our administrators in the Cayman Islands to wire the funds, they referred me to our bankers at Goldman, who referred me to our bankers in Geneva, who referred me to our bankers in Lichtenstein, who said I'd have to wait five days until they could find the funds to fund the wires, and that I'd have to get Peter's consent."

"What funds?"

"I don't know. It's never happened to me before. We usually have plenty of cash stashed in the Caymans to pay any redemption requests. I've only ever once gotten as far as Goldman, who sorted everything out within minutes. I didn't even know about the accounts in Geneva and Lichtenstein till I was referred there."

"So what did those guys tell you was happening?"

"Nothing. They can't."

"Why not?"

"I'm not authorized on those accounts. Only Peter is, apparently."

"What about the CFO?"

"There is no CFO. Peter is the CFO."

"Okay, well, that makes sense. If he's the CFO then only

he has the authority to wire." My level of knowledge impressed me. "But isn't it a huge red flag to have the CEO as the CFO?"

"Well, one guy asked about it once, but he was junior, and the head guys in Milwaukee fired him the next day after Peter chewed them out about it. He threatened to blacklist them."

"Hmm…" I reverted to my prior approach. Three more drinks arrived shortly thereafter.

When the server swished away again, Holton leaned in.

"I can't help but think, buddy, that there's something fishy going on, and it stinks."

"Fish does."

"Exactly. And this stinks like week-old sushi. What's worse is I'm going to be hung out to dry if there are any shenanigans going on."

"Like a pair of old lacrosse socks," I suggested.

"Exactly, man. There is something wrong with the system. I don't even know why I took this job. I should have been a trader like all my college buddies. That way you don't ever have to know what's going on behind the scenes."

"But you don't know what's going on."

"No, but I should. It's fucked up."

"The world is fucked up, Holton," I said profoundly.

"Exactly. We've got these guys at the top stealing from the rest of us." Apparently, there is nothing like the prospect of personal misfortune to turn a hedge funder into a socialist.

I felt I could add value here, so seized my chance. "You know, income inequality is at the highest level since the 1920s, or perhaps earlier." I had read it in the *Wall Street Journal* by mistake. "And we know what came next."

"You're right," said Holton feverishly. "The whole system is broken. Most people have no money, so they don't spend it. Because they don't spend what they don't have, the economy can't grow. Without the economy growing, there is no inflation. With no inflation, interest rates are low. Which forces the Federal Reserve to try to stimulate the economy by injecting money. That does nothing but drive up financial asset prices. But only the wealthy own financial assets, mostly billionaires. And billionaires don't spend much of their money because they are too busy trying to accumulate more than the other rich guys, and there are only so many two-hundred-foot yachts you can buy. So the economy stagnates, which keeps inflation and interest rates low, which forces the Fed to print more free money. Which inflates assets further. Which makes the rich richer and everyone else poorer."

"Perhaps they should market more three-hundred-foot yachts," I opined.

"It's no joke, Giles."

"I know. That's why I'm joking about it. Humor is the last refuge of despair, right? It's dead serious. It's the Catch-22 of the modern economy."

"More like the Snatch two and twenty, or three and thirty, Giles. Meanwhile, anyone with a talent or brain wants to become a hedge fund manager, as the only way of earning enough to live the American Dream is to feed off the scraps from the billionaire's table."

"And offer your wives as sacrificial lambs in their perverted fantasies," I remarked bitterly.

"Yeah, I thought that might happen," said Holton sadly. "I'm sorry. My wife can barely walk after a weekend at Peter's."

"At least she is willing to take one for the team," I consoled. "We ran away."

"You did? You're brave."

"No, just shit scared. What's worse is that the politicians

who are supposed to be protecting the people are in the pockets of the billionaires. The socialists are the worst."

"Bill Smith? That puffed-up pedo?"

"Yup. He couldn't get enough of the action. Bread and circuses for the people. Cash and concubines for him." I didn't dare ask more about Bill's perverse predilections.

"What are we going to do about it?" he asked passionately.

"I haven't the balls to do anything about it," I said honestly. "And I haven't earned enough to do something about it either."

"Nor have I," he said wistfully. "But maybe I should anyway?"

"Perhaps… Look, don't worry, Holton, my mum always said everything was for the best." I paused to reflect. "But then she died of ALS when I was six, paralyzed and being force-fed through a straw. At the end she couldn't even use her machine to talk to me in a computerized voice that sounded like Charlton Heston. So she may have been wrong."

"I'm sorry," he said earnestly.

"Not as sorry as I am."

We left the bar soon after. I'm not sure Holton got much out of our meeting, but I'd tried my best to cheer him up. As he put on his pathetic disguise to make his way out, he turned to me for a parting shot.

"By the way, I found out how you got hired."

"How?"

"One of the hookers in Peter's dungeon said she knew a stripper who she was sure he'd like. In one of their breaks, she played him some movie called *Princess Diaries, The King's Revenge.*"

"Thanks for telling me earlier, man," I replied angrily.

"I only found out yesterday," he said. I could tell he was being honest.

⮺

I left the bar unaffected by my conversation with Holton. If anything, I felt relieved that I was only responsible for Zyxview. He seemed to be bearing the weight of the whole system on his shoulders. He was a big guy, but no Atlas.

No sooner had I failed to hail a taxi than my phone vibrated in my thigh pocket. I let it ring a few times. It wasn't an unpleasant feeling.

"Son?" It was my father on the line.

"Yes, Father. What can I do for you?"

"*Eheu. Helga mortua est.*"

SIC TRANSIT HELGA MUNDI

HELGA'S FUNERAL WAS positively baroque: trumpets, choristers, and all. Fugues shook the pews, and sopranos challenged the stained-glass windows. No stop was left unpulled. It was exactly what Helga would have wanted.

The small Lutheran church in the West Village sweated Germans. Germans from New York, relatives from Germany, New Yorkers who spoke German. I would say it was as hot as an oven in there on that sultry August afternoon, but that would be in poor taste. At the least the service started bang on time.

Cherry sat in the front row next to Father, presumably because of her Germanic bloodline. Their Anglo friends (they had several) were right at the back. They didn't have any Jewish friends that I knew of, which is quite an achievement in New York. And other minorities would clearly have been beyond the pale.

My father opened the service somberly with the great Ecclesiastes 3. It lost some of its magic in German, especially as I only understood a couple of words. But the audience loved it. I could tell by the tears. "*Ein jegliches hat seine Zeit*," he intoned, almost as a Gregorian chant. He'd never really mastered German inflection. He would have been better off going for Latin, but I guess even he didn't have the guts to choose a Latin reading of the Bible in a Lutheran church.

Helga's time for dying came, it turned out, as the result of a massive pulmonary embolism triggered by a kosher frank-furter. If that isn't divine justice then I don't know what is. I'm sure the chain-smoking hadn't helped matters, poor woman. She'd had a bright future in academia, before my father saddled her with a nervous six-year-old who wet himself regularly after seeing his beloved mother expire before his eyes. I bore her no grudge. She raised me efficiently for seven whole years without so much as an itch. I credit my metamorphosis from abject despair to studied cynicism almost entirely to her and her occasional beatings. The English education merely set it in stone.

Several hymns and a lot of Bach later, I stood up to give the funeral address. My father thought it apposite that her only son (despite our lack of shared blood or bond) should be the one to send her on her way. I didn't want to disappoint him, so I said I would. My recent experiences at POS had put me in a particularly reflective mood, so it wasn't a bad call. I think he got more than he'd bargained for though. But hey, I was never going to see these people again, so I was free to speak from the heart. Cherry beamed wholesomely throughout.

"*Meine damen und herren*," I began, to much nodding and appreciation.

I peaked early.

"I hardly speak a word of German, so I am going to say a few words about my stepmother Helga, and my dad, Andrew, in Anglo Saxon German: that is, English. They usually communicated in Latin, but this will be *facilius* on everyone."

They looked confused, so I laughed, as Helga would have

done. It was meant to be a joke. They laughed in turn obediently. I immediately understood a lot more about the rise of the Third Reich.

"Helga, as you know, rescued my father from a midlife crisis following the death of my dear beloved mother. She wasn't much older than my mum, though she looked it." I laughed again. More laughter, though perhaps a bit less enthusiastic.

"Many of you may not know much about my father's background, least of all him." My father, sitting in the front row, was already looking ashen. And I'd only just begun. "You see, his mother was a Gypsy, and his great-grandfather, Andrew Goodenough I, was actually a Ukrainian Jew who arrived in the U.S. in the late nineteenth century after fleeing one of the more mundane Tsarist pogroms."

At this, some old relative of Helga's in the front pew started cackling to herself, and was joined by a handful of others nearby. Perhaps I'd stumbled upon the essence of German humor, though she may have just been Ribbentrop's niece, or not understood a word I was saying. At least the rest of the congregation had the good manners to mimic my stoic demeanor. Father lifted his head as if about to stand up, but thought better of it.

"In my research I have found no evidence of any Dukes of Escumesthorpe, let alone Dukes of Escumesthorpe called Goodenough. The most likely origin of our name Goodenough comes courtesy of my conversation with Solomon Goodenough of Queens, who told me his ancestors had also been given the last name Goodenough as a joke by the bureaucrats at Ellis Island, who, frustrated perhaps by a lost voice and Cyrillic papers, had said, 'Any old name is good enough.' Andrew was probably just one of their own names."

I laughed loudly. Only the old crone in the front row joined me. This is how the reformation must have begun.

"Andrew went on to work on a turkey farm in Virginia, where he married a Polish Jew called Rosa. It was his grandson, my father's father, Andrew Goodenough III, who broke free of the farm by inventing the now famed technique for force-feeding turkeys to achieve the ideal weight based on market dynamics in the run-up to Thanksgiving. He made a small fortune, most of which my father spent on himself and Helga. She liked a good car. A BMW, of course."

Someone in the back applauded briefly.

"Why this long detour about my father? Actually, I haven't the faintest idea. Perhaps I just thought most of you should know a bit about the man Helga married. Perhaps I've just been meaning to get it off my chest for a while.

"Now on to Helga, another immigrant to this great country of ours…"

The rest of my eulogy was less factual and more aspirational. What a wonderful classicist Helga was, what an incredible mother she had been to me in my times of need, how she would bake me and my friends little German cakes, how she always remembered my birthday, how she helped everyone she knew, was as loyal as a German shepherd (my rendition of *Deutscher Schaferhund* won me back some nods), and as playful as a Dachshund (I love animals).

I would never speak ill of the dead. Only the living.

I caught up with my father at the reception later. I apologized if I had caused him any distress, and said I hoped he could learn to live with both himself and me, now that Helga was gone. He didn't say anything to me other than "Et tu, Brute?" before downing yet another schnapps. It could have been worse.

"Wow, honey, that was quite the party," slurred Cherry, as we stumbled back home around midnight. Father had left early, and we'd spent the rest of the evening learning German drinking songs. "I do hope your dad is okay. He seemed totally upset. Helga meant so much to him. It's like so sweet. And those Germans are cray-zee."

I was glad she'd missed the point. It made me love her even more.

BACCHANALIA

ASIDE FROM NAGGING doubts about my father (who had gone to ground), the next couple of weeks passed without much ado about anything, let alone nothing.

Cherry started showing a little bump, though you'd only have noticed it if you were as well acquainted with her abs as I was. And she was even more horny than usual. Beyond that, she decided to throw herself an early baby shower in a week or so for her friends and followers, carefully selected by me to include no men except Hector and DeShaun. And her makeup line was prospering. Without my job and trust fund, she may have even been able to afford to rent a walk-up apartment in the Bronx, which for a millennial was the equivalent of a duplex on Fifth.

And work was bizarrely stable. Peter and I were in a truce. He didn't fire me even though there wasn't much of a rally in Zyxview stock. Two initiations at neutral were enough to provide a short-term base, it seemed. I think his mind was elsewhere. Or perhaps I'd thrown him by standing up to him. Or perhaps whatever had happened to Bertram was making him think twice about his next steps with me. Horton mentioned nothing about our conversation at the bar, so I assumed the issue had been cleared up. And Egon was on vacation in St. Tropez (it was reported in the gossip pages), jostling with various other billionaires for a prime mooring position in the harbor (there was a minor fracas). He had been seen on his yacht with several models (female), and rumor was that he'd gotten over his recent bust-up and moved on to the next page in the Victoria's Secret catalog. I wondered if he'd moved on from me too. I hoped so, but not so much as to have forgotten my advice.

∽

It was on an otherwise unremarkable Monday in early September, a couple of days before our scheduled baby shower, that the news finally hit, destroying the peace and sending a nuclear aftershock through the market.

It was timed perfectly, just as the final straggling billionaires had returned to their Bloombergs from the Hamptons and the Côte d'Azur, before using all their genius to make the perennial fall decision of whether to chase the markets higher into the year-end, or sell everything because everyone else was.

*PALO ALTO—Business Wire—Zyxview (Nasdaq: ZYX) announces upcoming announcement of announcement of several major products that will forever change humanity. On September 20th, Founder and CEO of Zyxview, Egon Crump, will take the stage at the SAP Center, San Jose, to give a keynote at the first annual Zyxview "Change The Future" festival. After performances from U2, The Rolling Stones, and Katy Perry, and speeches from visionaries such as Al Gore, Leonardo DiCaprio, and Bono, Mr. Crump will give a glimpse into all the major product lines that Zyxview is in advanced stages of developing, including products that will revolutionize mankind's answer to its imminent catastrophes, including Climate Change, Cancer & Infectious Diseases,

Famine, War, and Space Travel. "The world as we know it is f***ed," said Mr. Crump via Twitter this morning. "Our future as a species is dangling over a precipice. We at Zyxview are about to change that. Come join us at Change The Future if you give a sh*t about anything." Invitations to investors and ordinary people who care about the human race will be going out in the next few days. For inquiries please email Candy Carter, head of IR, at candy@zyx.com or text #yeswecan or #sisepuede to 4321.

I had to admit it. It was a fictional work of pure genius. Perhaps the greatest since the résumé I'd concocted for Merrill. And the market fell for it exactly as I'd expected it would. Trading in Zyxview was immediately halted. Shorts had been accumulating vast positions on the way down, as their thesis that it was going down was playing out. At the last check, its stock had 70 percent of its float short and was carrying a -40 percent borrow rate. Meanwhile, the best and brightest analysts on the sell-side had disowned it, then abandoned it, then beaten it with a spiked club when it was down.

No one had a Buy rating (let alone Conviction Buy), and it had fifteen Neutrals, ten Sells, and five Conviction Sells (or the equivalent). The new B of A analyst, Xander Thamrongnawasawat, had been the first to put a price target of zero on the stock. He had been hailed as a visionary over the last few weeks. Cramer had high-fived him twice on his show, and the other CNBC bobbleheads had been nodding at his unintelligible prognostications ever since.

The stock opened up 80 percent and was again halted. The atmosphere in the office was riotous. Traders fired Nerf blasters at each other deliriously; portfolio managers helicoptered wads of cash in all directions; and a squad of analysts covering Oil & Gas began twerking in unison toward my desk. Executive assistants stared me up and down salaciously like drunk MILFs at a Chippendale show; the IT guys sent everyone porn; and the lone person in the Compliance Department got so carried away that she twisted her ankle badly while attempting a backflip in front of Peter's desk and had to be carted off to the ER.

Peter just stared greedily at his screens, smiling, and even turned once to give me a thumbs-up. It brought back bad memories, but at least I knew he was probably close to orgasm. And I knew I was definitely in the clear. What he cared most about, at the end of the day, was money. And I was now making it for him. Lots of it. And I hadn't even had to break the law.

By the end of the day, the stock had rallied 150 percent, blasting through previous resistance to a new all-time high. It was the biggest one-day surge in a mid-cap stock people had seen in years. And that was only the start. Over the next week, the stock doubled again, as analysts fell over each other upgrading it back to Conviction Buy, in waves of convulsive, reflexive spasms of contrition and euphoria.

Poor Xander did his best. He broke down in tears on Cramer, who berated him for being so wrong while claiming he himself had known all along this was a "rocket-ship"; he quadruple upgraded the stock to his Best Ideas List, Certain Buy with a price target ten times above the recent low; and he even published a note on the likely songs The Rolling Stones would pick for the upcoming event. "(I Can't Get No) Satisfaction" wasn't on it—a rookie error that perhaps more than anything doomed his career to the same fate as Helga. He was fired without mercy.

In the meantime, I took the chaos as a golden opportunity to "work from home" for the rest of the week. I knew this thing was going a lot higher, so why gloat? By day two, when everyone realized that it was Peter and I who were going to be making the millions from this, I knew that the general euphoria would metastasize to visceral jealousy. There was a non-trivial chance that my life would be in danger if I set foot in POS. It's a long drop from the third-floor balcony.

Besides, I was surprised by how unelated I was by the whole circus. I won't lie: I was looking forward to the potential massive bonus. And it was nice to think I wasn't being thought of as a loser, or just "Lucky Jill." But that was as far as it went. Relief, contentment, calm. Nothing remotely approaching the jubilation I'd been expecting.

Perhaps it was just an anticlimax after all the anticipation. Perhaps I felt rightly that the whole damn thing was a sham. Perhaps it was my studied cynicism regaining its composure. Or perhaps it was the opposite. Perhaps—just perhaps—I had realized that there were more important things in life than others' perception of my success. Probably not, but perhaps. Whatever the reason, I am telling the truth when I say that I was far more excited about Cherry's baby shower that week than the surge in Zyxview's stock and my career.

Nor was the shower an anticlimax when it came.

∾

What had been originally conceived of as a gathering of close friends, family, and followers ended up (perhaps unsurprisingly) as a barnburner. Cherry's girlfriends brought girlfriends, our couple friends brought their couple friends, Hector and DeShaun brought more Hectors and DeShauns, and Instagram brought the rest.

Fortunately, the super shut it down successfully at around midnight with military tactics, or the entire floor might have given way. The elevator was deactivated, the front door to the building locked, and residents ushered up the emergency stairs while partyers were being ushered down. The NYPD held the perimeter and assisted where needed. The bill wasn't pretty, nor were the stares of my neighbors, but Cherry said it had been a "blast," and that's what mattered.

What's more, early in the evening, somewhere in between the impromptu beer pong tourney in our kitchen and the first semi-nude Twister round robin in our bedroom (which Cherry won, by the way), my father dropped by. Much to my surprise, he was in a fantastic mood, though it took me a while to find out, as I was arm wrestling Hector at the time in the pantry.

"I miss Helga," he said as we sipped champagne in the master bathroom, the only place we could find even a modicum of calm. "But I've been thinking a lot about what you said at her funeral."

"Not too much, I hope," I said nervously. It was awkward enough conducting a conversation from the toilet seat, let alone as profound a one as this was clearly going to be.

"You can never think too much, Giles. You know that. And I've been doing some real thinking, about who I am and what matters, and it has liberated me in a way. I won't claim to have been blinded by a light on the Road to Damascus, but I'm certainly starting to see things around me in a different hue."

"That's good, Father," I said soothingly, as if I were the father and he my son. "My method was clumsy, I know, but I couldn't think of a better way."

"Well, there probably wasn't a worse way." We both smiled. "But then perhaps it was the only way. You see, I knew snippets about my ancestors, not the whole story. It was your granddad who brought me up to believe I was something special, something I wasn't; and perhaps my love for the perceived purity of Greece and Rome encouraged me to adhere to the tenets of the false narrative. I am at heart a romantic who wants to believe that there are eternal truths and superior forms of human existence. It's a way of escaping the mediocrity of mortality, I suppose. I think that's what attracted your mother to me in the first place, and Helga, though perhaps in a less saintly way."

"We are all works-in-progress, I guess," I said, offering a truism to ease the emotion.

"Your mother loved you very much, you know," he continued, refusing to bite. "She was an innocent, sweet child. Pure. That's why I loved her. She had a genuine affection for people that I envied. She died far too young, collateral damage to all our imperfections. *Tantaene animis caelestibus irae*?"

And with that he began to cry. I hugged him and cried too. We'd both probably already had a bit too much champagne.

"I love you, Dad."

"I love you, son." We embraced for the first time in years.

"Yo, faggots, stop ramming each other in there. I need to piss." Some jackass was trying to kick the door down. It turned out it was one of Cherry's transgender friends. Apparently, they are allowed to say things like that.

And that's where we left things.

I know Dad stayed for a while longer, because I caught sight of him from a distance around 9 p.m., shotgunning beers on the fire escape with a midget called Jasper who had been in one of Cherry's movies (as an extra, I should add). After that, I lost track of him. I was occupied elsewhere, mostly trying to turn back the waves of new arrivals like some modern-day Cnut. I was equally successful, as you've heard. The party got progressively wilder as I got progressively more sober, which is never a good dynamic. I even had to stop a guy called Larry (undoubtedly @dirtylarry69) from doing coke off the bottom of a crib that someone had brought as a present. He graciously removed himself to my bedside table.

"Well, that was something," I said to Cherry as the last of the cop cars pulled away.

"What a rager!" She laughed, seemingly having managed to enjoy every minute of it despite being stone-cold sober.

"This may take a few weeks to clean up."

"Or a few months, honey!"

"Well, I suppose it was worth it, to send our childless life off with one final blowout," I said, neither convincingly nor convinced.

"You know, I was like thinking the same thing, sweetie. This probably marks the end of an era. It's time to like settle down a bit, isn't it?"

"Yeah, I guess so," I sighed, holding her close. "But not completely. We're going to be parents, not geriatrics."

"Is there a difference?"

"Not much, I'm afraid. But I'm kind of looking forward to it."

"Me too," she said, winking. "But not before I give *you* one final blowout."

"It better not be the last!" I sniggered as she pushed me down onto the sofa.

"You scratch my back and I'll scratch yours," she purred.

THE FUTURE PERFECT

"BUT I STILL haven't found what I'm looking for. Thank you, San Jose!"

U2 wrapped up their set.

"Give it up for U2! Give it up for Bono!" whooped Egon, cartwheeling onto center stage from behind the drums. Clearly acrobatic talent was inherited. "He's a fucking legend! What a great man, what an ambassador for the future, and he's done it all *pro bono*."

My father would have pointed out that that could be translated in various ways, including "for the benefit of Bono," but I neither wanted to be churlish at this stage in the festivities, nor had anyone in the arena who would have understood the pun. Tom was an engineer.

"You've got to give it to Egon—he sure knows how to put on a circus," screamed Tom over the din, while fist-pumping the air.

"It runs in the family," I shouted back. Tom nodded. He had clearly read the Wikipedia entry too.

You may be surprised by Tom's magnanimous enthusiasm. It turns out Fin had covered their short position near the recent bottom, and they were waiting for a good opportunity to re-short. "It's still a fraud," he had told me over a hot dog at lunchtime, "but like all frauds, there's a time for shorting and there's a time for covering."

"How biblical," I observed. And how impressive. He really understood this company better than anyone, and had managed to break even so far, despite being wrong about the stock. He had showed me some of his analysis. It was voluminous, brilliant (I think—I only understood half of it), and far too much like hard work. He was fighting a lonely battle. How much simpler to just be long, and make a ton of money before anyone discovered Tom was dead right. Given the recent ascent it was clear that any awakening might be years away.

"I hope you're enjoying yourselves," yelled Egon to the crowd. A few people shouted back, "Yeah!"

"I said I hope you're enjoying yourselves!"

"Yeah," roared back the crowd in unison. For an instant I had flashbacks to Helga's funeral. God, people in groups are stupid.

"But now it's time to get serious, so take your seats and turn on your brains. Give me ten minutes and I will give you the answers you've been looking for." Dry ice billowed from beneath Egon, and a gigantic screen emerged from behind him where the band had been. The crowd simmered down as the stadium lighting dimmed. A video began to play on the screen. In 4K ultra HD, of course.

What followed turned the excitement into tears. There was footage of a polar bear trapped by the melting sea ice; of children in Africa trying to pump a dry well; of a bald young girl in a hospital ward struggling to stay alive; of traffic belching exhaust fumes on a Los Angeles highway; of hurricanes, tornadoes, earthquakes, and tsunamis, with families searching for life in the rubble; of a rocket launching into space with *Mars 2040: Our Last Hope* emblazoned on it; of nuclear weapons being detonated and the recreation of the nuclear winter sure to follow. It ended by zooming into the blue eyes of a toddler, alone on a blackened tree stump, in the middle of a burnt-out wood, looking forlorn and confused (as she no doubt was by the entire video shoot). There wasn't a dry eye in the house. Even Tom looked moved.

"That, ladies and gentlemen, is what we have to look forward to," intoned Egon somberly as the lights came back on. Behind him on the screen was a single word: "Zyxview," set over pictures of smiling children and green fields. "Unless we…"

"CHANGE! NOW!" screamed the assembled masses. They'd been set up for this throughout the day. Even the hot dog stands and carnival attractions had been adorned with various signs carrying the slogan *Change! Now!*

"Fuck yeah," screamed Egon back at them, with his sincerest "fuck" to date. "And who is going to change it?" he caterwauled, pointing at the screen.

"Zyxview!" shrieked the audience.

"Zyx-view, change! Zyx-view, change! Zyx-view, change!" he ululated rhythmically, pumping a closed right fist into the air on every "change."

The whole audience of sheeple followed, desperately attempting to synchronize their pumps and outdo the person next to them in slavish zeal. The decibel level reached fever pitch on about the twentieth "change." These maniacal morons put the Nuremburg rallies to shame, I couldn't help but think. Even Tom and I started pounding the air while exchanging wide-eyed stares with each other. We didn't want to get thrown out. I could have sworn Egon turned to me and winked. It was improbable though. He was a long way away. He may have just blinked.

Egon stopped suddenly and lowered his gaze. He waited patiently. Within a minute there was total silence. I looked around and noticed most of the audience was staring at the ground in sympathy.

"Comrades in the fight…fellow travelers on our journey to liberation…friends," began Egon soberly. "We at Zyxview have long held that we cannot look back to the future. We must look forward, our heads held high." He lifted his head and gazed out at the masses. They lifted theirs and gazed back. The unthinking sycophancy was mesmeric.

"We cannot rely on the old approaches and older platitudes. We must fundamentally revolutionize our approach to the challenges we all face. We are the human race. We are one people. We are one company."

"Zyx-view, change!" someone in the front row screamed, leaping to their feet and pumping the air. It may have been Al Gore. His neck was almost as thick as his shoulders. Everyone else followed. When the brief outburst had rippled to a standstill, Egon continued, looking both paternal and mystical (he was wearing a hooded robe, and had grown a massive beard for the occasion, looking something like a cross between Obi-Wan Kenobi and a Dominican friar).

"Fuck the past! Fuck wrong! Fuck profit! Fuck imperialism! Hail the future! Hail right! Hail equality! Hail brotherhood!" Another minute of deranged "Zyx-view, change!" chanting, interspersed with an occasional "fuck" and "hail."

"So…now the moment you have all been waiting for," said Egon, flatly. "The moment I tell you what we are going to do about it. The moment your understanding of what's possible changes. You will tell your grandchildren you were here, in the vanguard of our army of love, when we announced the announcement of our products that will cure the world of its ills. Otherwise, your grandchildren may not make it past childhood."

The audience sat forward in their seats, legs quivering in excitement.

"First, we will solve climate change…" Behind him on the screen the toddler on the tree stump reappeared, looking around her in awe as the trees began to regrow and the forest thicken. Animals scampered at her feet, and a lady, obviously her mother, ran and picked her up, lifting her into the air in joy. Suddenly, an assembly line could be seen. Happy workers in ZYX-tagged polo shirts high-fived each other as they took what appeared to be sleek, iPad-sized units off a production line, and stared at them in feigned wonder.

"…with one simple device. Zyx-view, change!" screamed Egon to the crowd. The crowd didn't disappoint.

"Then," he continued, when the latest bout of mania had subsided, "we will banish cancer and infectious diseases to the hellhole they came from." Video of the bald girl throwing off her bedsheets, and then running through a field of poppies with a full head of hair. Children with scabrous lesions that became whole as if by magic. Africans used mosquito nets to fish in deep, gushing rivers. And so on, you get the idea. More of the happy assembly line. Pause. Silence.

"…with one simple device. Zyx-view, change!" More delirium.

"We will feed the world." Videos of starving children, now healthily rotund, eating fresh fish from plates overloaded with bright vegetables.

"…with one simple device. Zyx-view, change!"

"Begone, war!" More videos.

"…with one…"

"Simple device. Zyx-view, change!" chanted the crowd, as the camera zoomed in on a different iPad-sized device. At least it was a different color. It was a green box, rather than the previous red box. Beyond that its features were the same indecipherable mash-up of screens, buttons, antennae, and holes. It looked like something out of *Star Trek*. I'm sure no one else was paying the slightest attention to it.

"Now," said Egon humbly, "not everything can be done with just one simple device. For space travel you are going to need your own…" Drumroll…"space travel machine… Who wants one?"

"Me…us…I do…fuck yeah…" the baying mass screeched. If someone had said "no" they would likely have been flayed alive. I joined in with a half-hearted "you bet!"

And then it emerged from below the stage: a futuristic monstrosity, somewhere between the Apollo 11 landing craft and a *Star Wars* X-wing starfighter. There was so much smoke billowing around it that it was impossible to make out much more than its outline. Then, unlike the screaming that accompanied its revelation, it was back down again in a flash. The crowd stomped, the crowd whistled, the crowd howled, the crowd fist-pumped. Several people fainted and had to be removed on stretchers.

"Fuck yeah, baby!" Egon shouted, arching his back and pointing to the roof. "That's god's work that is. God's a fucking legend! We've done it! Thank you, St. Jose! Thank you, Leonardo, Katy, Mick, Al, Bono, all of you who care about Change, Now! God bless the USA! God bless this earth!"

The dry ice billowed again, and Egon adopted a Black Panther pose as he was slowly lowered below the stage.

"We Are the Champions" blared, disco lights wheeled,

and strobes flashed (another couple of people were stretchered out)—it was all as predictable as it was predictably effective in our meme-crazed world. The assembled masses climaxed.

It ended just as Egon would have wanted. Katy Perry ran on stage singing "Firework." Someone mistook the accompanying explosions for a machine gun. There was a stampede. Ten people were crushed to death. And the entire event dominated media coverage for days. It was pure Americana. Even Donald Trump was jealous, apparently.

MANIAS, PANICS, AND...

"YOU AN INVESTOR then?" asked my South Asian taxi driver on the way back from JFK (I still hadn't downloaded Uber or Lyft).

Unfortunately, I'd committed the cardinal error of not leaving my earbuds in after the flight, which had given him the all-clear to begin peppering me with personal questions as soon as he had turned on the meter and locked the doors to prevent my escape. What's worse, despite the odds, he spoke some English. I cursed my rare misfortune, but at least his AC was working.

"Um, I wouldn't go that far," I replied honestly, hoping to stop him in his tracks. It had no chance of working.

"You heard of *Zyxview*?" Jesus, even the taxi drivers.

"Oh yeah, I read about that. Probably worth avoiding. Seems like hype." I didn't want to be responsible for ending this guy's retirement dreams.

"Reeally? That's not what Jim Cramer say. You know, the guy on TV. He say it best stock out there. Love that guy. He very funny man."

"Funny if you like losing money," I replied sardonically. He didn't get it.

"Booyakasha, booka," he chanted with a chuckle, sizing me

up in the rearview mirror. "He a Jew. Jews very clever. Control whole world. You must listen to him." I ignored his casual anti-Semitism. "I going buy more in my E-Trade. Already make many dollars. I buy last week. I will be retire soon."

"Well done," I said as dismissively as I could. "Sorry, man, I've gotta take a call."

I put my earbuds in and pretended to talk to someone for the rest of the hour-long trip. It required a lot of creative fakery. Egon would have been proud.

⤢

Cherry was waiting for me back at home. Her bump looked a little rounder than when I left, but I may have been imagining it. She embraced me lovingly, then took my hand off her ass and put it on the bump.

"Can you believe it, honey?" she gasped gently.

"It's kicking," I replied in wonder.

"*Our* baby."

"I hope so," I said, smiling.

"Me too." She laughed. "I just hope it's as smart as its daddy. Hector told me that Zyxview is going crazy. Everyone is buying some. I even saw it on my Instagram feed. Someone's kid is dying and they are hoping that the new product comes out in time to save it. Do you think it will?"

I felt positively filthy by association. I tried to stay positive. Maybe Egon really did have these hypothetical products and all I had done was encourage him to announce them. Perhaps he had my number from the start, and this bravado about doing nothing was just a show to throw Wall Street off its game. I couldn't rule it out. Stranger things have happened, right? If necessity is the mother of invention, then shame is the father of delusion.

"I hope so," I replied neutrally.

"It would be so wonderful, handsome. Then not only would you make like a lot of money so baby and I can live like royalty, but you will have been part of something like so meaningful."

"All is for the best. Right?" I quipped.

She knew my mother's favorite phrase by heart. "Bestest ever!" she enthused.

I liked it. "In the bestest of all possible worlds."

A few weeks later, in early October, Zyxview announced its massive $20B secondary offering. The stock had doubled again going into and coming out of the "Change The Future" event. It was up eightfold since the bottom and fourfold since we'd bought it. With a market cap of $250B, it was now one of the largest companies in the USA. And with hundreds of millions of underwriting fees on the line, the banks fell over themselves promoting its potential to anyone left who didn't know it was the biggest thing since the Big Bang.

Peter's excitement following the announcement of the announcement had now faded into smug satisfaction. At least that's what I thought it was. He said very little, even when the stock rallied day after day. As a result the office was quiet and I got fewer stares of hate, though as my expected bonus kept rising exponentially, I had to keep my wits about me.

We didn't participate in the secondary. We didn't need to. The stock only fell about 10 percent on the announcement and was making new highs by the time the new shares began trading the next day. There were plenty of taxi drivers left to draw in, it seemed.

"I'm going to sell some," Peter told me when he called me

down soon after. "This has been a run for the history books. If only you'd done the right thing when you came to visit me at the castle, your bonus would have been more than the fifty million you are looking at now."

He winked.

"Wow!" I said. "I'll take that trade-off. Thank you."

"Don't thank me. Thank yourself. It probably won't matter anyway," he said with a strange humility that was deeply unsettling.

"How come?" I asked cautiously.

"Fuck off, Giles," he replied enigmatically. I retreated to my desk, followed furtively by Holton.

"Hey, man, let's go get some fresh air," he said as innocently as he could. He badly needed some lessons from Dawn. But then so had Bertram.

⚜

Holton and I shot the shit meaninglessly on the way to Bryant Park.

"Okay, I think we are safe here," he said at last, taking a bench rendered invisible from almost every direction by a wall and the fetid clouds of smoking fat which emanated from an adjacent kebab cart.

"What's up, big man?" I asked, feeling conspiratorially close to Holton.

"This," he responded. "This is up, down, and all over me." He untucked his shirt and lifted it just enough to reveal a patchwork of wires. I puckered.

"You're wearing a wire!" I shouted moronically.

"Shut the fuck up, dude," he shouted. "What's wrong with you? Quiet."

I didn't point out the fact that my shout was completely

drowned by the music blaring from the cart. It sounded like the soundtrack from one of those jihadi training videos. Such are our prejudices—even mine, and I don't think of myself as having any, let alone many.

"I didn't notice it," I whispered.

"What?" he shouted.

"I didn't notice," I said at conversational volume, pointing at his waist.

"No, of course you didn't. That's the idea. They keep the unit out of sight. Most of it is in my rectum."

"Nice," I said with a smirk.

"Not my thing, dude. Not that I have anything against it."

"I didn't mean it like that. I meant it's cool technologically. What's going on?"

"Well, let's just say that the Feds have woken up to the fact that POS needs a deeper look."

"And you're giving it to them by letting them get a deeper look inside you."

"Yup. I don't want any part of this shit… You know those new hires I made in the back office?"

"Of course not," I replied honestly.

"Let's just say they aren't just working for Peter."

"Fuck."

"Fuck is right. This is big. But you and I are safe. You've got nothing to do with this." I unpuckered, which was more than Holton could do, I supposed. "Keep your head down, that's all. I just wanted to let you know that now is the time to maintain a safe distance from Peter."

"Sure, dude," I answered, wondering who was listening on the other end. "I hardly even know the guy," I added for insurance.

"I know," he said with a wink. "You're virtually brand new, and are just doing your analysis."

"Yup. Just working away modeling and analyzing," I lied.

"Keep it that way."

"I will."

⤙

As I walked back home from Bryant Park (there was no way I was going back to the office, probably ever), I wondered what all this meant. Was my $50M bonus under threat the day I'd been promised it? Did I care? How much? Did Peter know what was going on? What was Holton up to? I felt fairly confident it couldn't be about Zyxview. What about the suspicious deaths of POS employees? What about the wires from the administrator? Or the underage kids at his orgies? Or something else? It was hard to know what to think. My phone interrupted both my wondering and wandering. An unknown caller. I usually ignored these types of inbound inquiries, but something impelled me to pick up.

"Dude, what's up?"

It was Egon. Was this being recorded too?

"Hey, Egon, how are you doing?"

"Where's the love, man?"

"What do you mean?"

"I mean that I haven't heard from you for fucking ages. What did you think of the event?"

"It was incredible, Egon," I answered truthfully. "I'm about to get onto a subway," I continued untruthfully. "How can I help you?"

"I want you to come see me...or at least see me and come." He cracked himself up.

"You know I don't feel that way about you," I replied, as

casually as I could while tightening up in a panic. Nothing good could come from this, whatever he was talking about.

"Brosephus, relax. You sound stressed. I have the perfect break for you. I'm sending a plane. I want to show you what's happening with Peach. Don't worry, it's got nothing to do with Zyxview. Be at Jet Aviation at Teterboro at 6:30 this evening. Dawn will look after you."

"Okay," I replied limply, and hung up. I felt I had no choice. All was going to be for the bestest, right?

...ALTITUDE?

"WOW, IT LOOKS incredible, Egon."

"What?"s

"That thing with the wheels."

"There are several of those in here, idiot. Which one?"

"That one."

I was pointing at something in a large floor-lit display cabinet at the far end of the hangar, sandwiched between a G650 and several Ferraris. It was pretty dark in there, but that was all I could see that was remotely unusual. And I was expecting something very unusual. The Peach, whatever it was, if it even existed. The jewel in the crown of the eponymous company that Zyxview was hypothetically about to spend its fresh stash of cash acquiring.

Dawn had arrived at dusk. She'd picked me up from the FBO disguised as Bill. I'm not sure why that was necessary, as the Global Express we boarded had a gold *ZYX* the size of a whale emblazoned on its matte-black fuselage. I guess you can never be too careful. And I still to this day don't know how she apes such a deep baritone, but I do know that she likes Pringles, as she went through at least five boxes on our flight to an undisclosed location deep in the Nevada desert, while I watched *Game of Thrones* on a king-sized waterbed.

One thing is for sure. Environmentalists sure know how to travel in style while saving the world.

"Hey d-bag," said Egon, flipping a switch to light up the entire hangar like his interrogation room back at HQ, and simultaneously smacking my ass with a contact that lingered considerably longer than when we had first met. Or was it just my imagination? "That, Mr. Just-In-Enough, is a Segway. You think I'd build something like that? The guy that bought the company drove off a frigging cliff in one. I mean what a loser. Fucking a-hole must have realized he'd just bought something that was ten years after its time before its time, if you get me."

"Yes, of course. Sorry. But why's it gold? I never saw a gold Segway."

"Because they gave me one when they were trying to sell me the company. In a dumb-ass display case too. I kept it to remind me what I never wanted to become like. A golden fossil. A golden relic. A golden piece of proto-history. A golden reverse Midas touch. A piece of golden turd. Capisce?"

I knew better than to answer back when he went Godfather on me. "Got it. Sorry."

"Stop fucking apologizing. What's the frigging matter with you? You are such a little British schoolgirl at heart. All prim and proper and uptight. Pull that pole out of your ass, and stick a dick up there, cowgirl. Preferably mine."

Recent weeks had apparently inflated more than just his inflated ego to bursting point, and I was still a target, despite the new model girlfriends. At least he didn't mention love.

"Sure, Egon," I whispered pathetically as I trotted after him across the hangar.

We had just passed the Segway when he stopped, turned, and grabbed hold of my arms.

"Okay, now turn around for me."

"What?"

"Relax, Mr. Moneypenny," Egon professed in his best Sean Connery brogue, "you won't feel a thing." He burst out laughing, slowly morphing it into an exaggerated Dr. Evil guffaw. He was like some third-rate YouTube impression channel. Not that I was going to tell him—I was too busy puckering up as usual.

"I'm going to need to blindfold you," he stated in a dead-pan voice. "Turn around."

"What?"

"There are more words than *what* in the English language, Justin…" He paused for dramatic effect, staring even deeper into my eyes, as if we were back at HQ. "Like big…thick… and veiny."

I was on the cusp of peeing now. I hadn't been as terrified since the prefect and broom incident at boarding school, despite all my recent traumas. I gulped, audibly.

"Your brain, dude," he snorted. "Relax. Your brain is big and veiny, but you are thick, dumb, a moron basically. Seriously, Jill, stop resisting. I'm just going to blindfold you till I get you in The Peach. There are some things I don't want you to see."

I turned around at last. I didn't have a choice really. It was awful. "Okay" was the best I could muster. As he slipped some type of cloth over my eyes, I felt his breath way too close to my neck, and his loins even closer to my backside. I was about to channel *Law and Order: SVU*, and reverse-kick him as hard as I could in his family jewels. But he backed off just in time.

Putting his hands on my shoulders, he guided me forward. I heard a door open, and then we must have moved into a new room in the hangar because the light level shifted down significantly. After about another fifty steps he stopped me.

"Ready to mount it?" he asked with a snigger.

"What?" I asked stupidly. It was the stress.

"What? What? What? The Peach, you retard. *What* I brought you here to see. Something that is going to change the world as we know it and make me an even richer stupendously rich man, maybe the richest ever, a kind of Da Vinci–Rockefeller–Gates combo. The first trillionaire. Bezos on crack. Four commas, baby. You know the plan."

"Jesus, Egon, yes, of course I'm ready to see it. Do you have a prototype?"

"No, sorry, Jill," Egon whispered apologetically.

"What do you mean?" I asked, disappointed. Was everything just BS? A huge joke at my expense? I wouldn't have been that surprised. A man who promises everything and delivers nothing is hardly a guy to rely on for something.

"Just what I said. What you hear is what you get. There is no model. There is just the final fucking product."

With that he began to push me up some small steps as I gasped out questions.

"What do you mean the final product? That can't be possible. I assumed there would be years of development, testing, and refinement. You don't mean the actual fully equipped, ready-to-sell version? You mean Zyxview is going to hypothetically buy a company with an actual product?"

I was genuinely concerned for him. That had never been his strategy. At least I hadn't thought it was. Perhaps I'd misunderoverestimated him, to paraphrase Dubya.

"You may think that. I couldn't possibly comment."

What could it be? The possibilities were now running through my mind. My panic was turning to excitement. I heard something click next to us. *It sounds like a vehicle door opening.* And with that Egon untied the blindfold.

"There's my PEACH, baby!" Egon shouted, hysterically jumping up and down on the step below me. "My peachy Peach. My Personal Electric Autonomous Computerized Helicopter! The biggest fucking revolution in transportation since Henry Ford woke up with a wrench and had an extra cup of coffee. Get in. We're going for a ride."

I was at the rear carbon fiber hatch of what seemed like a dark-colored Perspex and glass pod, shaped somewhere between a cube and an egg. Leaning back a bit, I could see in the dim light that it was about ten feet by ten at the base, and at least eight feet at the apex. I could just make out little aerodynamic wings on the outside of the pod, and helicopter-style rotor blades attached above it.

"It looks more like a giant pineapple than a peach," I said facetiously, still trying to get my bearings. "What are you going to call it?"

"Peach, you idiot. Perhaps *The Peach*."

"But that's the codename."

"It is also the name." Egon chortled. "Brilliant, right? Peach, as in *James and the Giant Peach*. It will fly you away by magic from your daily troubles to the land of your dreams. In minutes." He paused, almost sighing with delight at the brilliance of his own imagination. "My parents would have fucking loved it. All circus-folk are escapists. Some literally, figuratively, *and* metaphorically."

He paused, lost in his thoughts, memories, or ego. Or maybe a combination of the three. "Anyhow, what the fuck. Who gives a shit what the name is, sweetheart?" he barked out at last, reverting to his carefully constructed frat boy persona. "This is going to change the world, change our lives, and all you can think about is the name. That's why I'm the real genius and you are just another little bloodsucking cocksucker and wannabe genius. Get in."

With that he pushed me through the door.

Inside, The Peach was as commodious as the plane I'd just flown in on, with three rows of single, double-width, lie-flat leather seats either side of a central plushly carpeted aisle. Ahead of the front two seats was a massive glass window that ran from the apex of the pod down to a wide-screen monitor that stretched around the base of the front half of the vehicle. Looking out of the window, I could just about see that The Peach was sitting in some kind of small garage. It was dark but I could make out posters on the wall and a lot of robotic machinery all around us.

"Incredible" was the only thing I could think to say.

"You ain't seen nothing yet, sonny Jim." Egon cackled, steering me into the front right seat, while he crashed down in the seat across the aisle. "Get ready for the ride of your life. First things first, though."

With that he pressed the monitor in front of him, which immediately came to life. I couldn't make out all the buttons and functions. It looked like a giant scientific calculator, EKG machine, and airplane dashboard all melded into one. I gripped the armrests on my seat, expecting us to lurch forward immediately, but instead all that happened was that a table emerged from the floor between us.

"Time to christen this baby. Get ready to blow everything: your mind, my blow, and my dick. Ha ha!"

While I deciphered Egon's innuendo, he took out a cigarette case from his jacket.

"I didn't know you smoked," I observed in a bewildered voice. Smoking in Silicon Valley was considered worse than murder, rape, and pillage, combined.

"I don't. Well, except for crack. Occasionally. I prefer to inhale the pure powder."

Egon swiveled his seat toward the table and then helped me do the same by releasing a catch in the armrest. Facing me he opened the cigarette case and tipped out a huge mound of white powder. Given the context, it was pretty clear this was the Colombian marching kind. I just stared. It was hard to think of anything, relevant or even irrelevant, to say.

"I'll go first, how about that," said Egon, forming himself a huge white line that ran the length of the table with a credit card. "Time to get as high as this kite." Taking a metal straw out of the cigarette case, he took it down in one long snort.

I'll be honest. I was impressed.

He lifted his head and took a long, hard look at me. I saw his pupils dilating right before my eyes. I thought he might collapse there and then. But he exhaled dramatically and handed me the straw. "Come on now, your turn, mofo."

"Egon, seriously, I'm not sure about this. I mean I've experimented with coke before back at college, but I've never done anything like this. You took down a gram in one line."

"Baby baby baby boy, don't worry, man, I'm not going to give you anything like that, just a little to open you up. I need to tell you something, bro. I need you to listen to me. I need your love—all you need is love da da da-da-da, all you need is love da da da da-da-da, all you need is love, love, love is all you need."

The drugs were clearly working. No one sang The Beatles while on coke unless they'd gone uber-large. And love was back on the table. You know by now my autonomic reaction.

Egon finished his manic tapping with the credit card, and in front of me lay two rails of cocaine, gigantic by my estimation, but Lilliputian next to what he had just voraciously insufflated into one nostril. I surmised it was improbable that I could do them both without risking cardiac arrest, but there was also nowhere to run or hide. As if to emphasize this point, Egon had just tapped some more buttons and the rear hatch had slammed shut.

"It's just the two of us now, baby…oh yeah, just the two of us. Peachy, play 'Just the Two of Us.'"

"Sure, Egon" came a voice across the audio system. It was so realistic I thought Charlton Heston had been reincarnated and was sitting behind me. I even turned to check.

"I chose that just for you, man, just for you, just for us, just for time, for love, so good, Charlton, I mean, you can choose any voice," Egon said, in one enormous river of consciousness.

"I'm happy with Charlton," I responded in between snorts, as the Grover Washington hit started its smooth beat. "It reminds me of my mom. Her dying voice. Let's go somewhere, man. Isn't that why we're here?"

"Of course, Jill. Peachy, take us to point A."

The coke hit me at the same time as the garage doors opened. Within seconds my brain and body were silently elevating. I was flying. Deaf and dumb. As high as a kite. Silently. Higher to the stars, nothing underneath, darkness all around, floating and dreaming, but so much better than imagination. My heart fluttered like a butterfly with hummingbird wings, and my nerves tingled like thousands of hailstones blown against a foil curtain. It was a poetic moment, okay?

"Where are we going, Egon?" I asked when my power of speech had finally returned.

"To point A, sweetheart."

"Where's point A?"

"Nearer than point B, further than point C. Up, up, and away."

"Who's flying it?"

"Charlton Heston."

"Really? I thought he was dead."

"He is."

"That's amazing."

A brief moment elapsed.

"Giles?" said Egon seriously.

"Yes."

"I love you. I know you know that but now I really love you. Like love love, not just sex love. I'll make a trillion dollars and give it all to you. I already have. You can have whatever you want. I'll buy you boats, cars, planes, peaches, clothes, girls, anything."

"Shit, Egon. I still don't feel that way about you. I wish I did. I don't want your money. I don't want any money, I don't think. Or just enough, I guess. Okay, give me a bit. But I don't do gay. God, it would be awesome to be gay. Or better bisexual. I'd love it. Twice the options, two squared, cubed, to infinity. So many guys love me. I'd love to love your love. So Classical. Like Athens and Rome. Purity of love and all that."

I have no idea if I meant what I was babbling. I was in a world where nothing made any sense, and everything made none.

"Please, Giles. You're the only person I could ever really be happy with. I love love love love love you," he pleaded.

"No, Egon. I said no. Okay?"

From his face it clearly wasn't okay.

"Fuck you then," he said suddenly, grounding my high with a gravitational bluntness. The stars seemed to begin to fall toward us. The Peach constricted. I felt choked. "If you won't love me, then no one will; if you don't understand me, then no one can; if you won't learn, then I will teach, school, educate, and discipline you with my grim reaper. Without love there's no point; without a point there is no beginning and no end. Only nothingness—where my parents are, and where I'm taking you and my Peach with me.

"Peachy, destruct."

"Egon, what the fuck?" I screamed. My butterfly heart became a strangled ball of energy. My tingling brain started thudding. Charlton started shouting at us in gobbledygook about altitude, vectors, velocity, patterns, programs, and overrides. Egon kept giving him codes and confirmations.

"I'm taking your love with me to the grave, Jill. Unfortunately, I can't detach you from it. I can't make you my mommy if you won't be my daddy. I can't redo the beginning if you won't do my end. Turning back is pointless when you won't turn your back forward."

He continued to jabber meaningless paradoxes. And then it happened. We began to fall. Slowly at first, like when you get to the top of a roller coaster and peek over the edge and the first car starts to crest and you know what is coming.

I unbuckled and fell off the seat onto my knees. "Please, Egon, please abort the abortion. I will blow your mind and body. I will learn to love your love. Cherry will be fine with it. We have an open relationship."

"Too late, buddina," screamed Egon manically. "Too late. I'm going down like Major Kong, straddling my babies." He shoveled the remaining mound of coke into his face and jumped on top of me. He was riding me like a Harley as we picked up the pace of our descent. I couldn't shake him, and it was too late anyway.

My final memory is of his weight on my back, brief

flashes of Mum, Cherry's tits, Dad, my unborn child (who for some reason looked like an American Girl doll), and then Egon's crazed voice singing the Hallelujah Chorus from Handel's Messiah.

I don't know why I've spent all my life worrying about death. It's the moment before that's far more disturbing, apparently.

Then nothingness. If that isn't your worst nightmare come true, then you're luckier than me, which is hard to imagine, as I survived the crash.

SURPRISE!

I AWOKE TO find my father reading Horace in a chair at the side of my bed.

"Good morning, Dad," I muttered hoarsely.

"Good morning, son," my father replied soothingly, getting up to stroke my hair. "You're finally back with us in the land of the living. Charon wouldn't let you pass, though he thought long and hard. For three months, in fact. But I refused to give you the obol."

"Thanks for that, Dad. But I quite liked the land of the dead. Good views," I said honestly, thinking of the nun again.

"*Aegri somnia vana*; nothing more, I'm afraid, old chap."

"Well, at least they were good dreams, for the most part."

"That's comforting to know. Meanwhile, here on *terra firma* there is much news. But I'm not sure you are ready for the whole story. It may affect your bowel movements."

"How's Cherry?" I asked, suddenly aware that she wasn't there.

"She is a proud mother, and you, apparently, are the proud father of a lovely little girl. She is actually in the maternity ward. Your baby is but a day or two old. She knows you are coming out of the coma, fully intact, though it may take a while for you to be able to walk again. Your muscles have atrophied." I wiggled my toes. I tried to move my legs but the effort was too much still. "Otherwise, all the tests suggest you are *mens sana in corpore sano*."

"And Egon?"

"A goner. He was found underneath you, legs around your body, shielding you from the impact, no doubt. A brave soul."

As you know, I didn't generally speak ill of the dead, so I just nodded. I guess he died where he wanted to be. We must have rolled over in the final few moments.

"Now rest, son," my father continued. "There is much more to tell you, but the doctors say you must rest a while longer. There is nothing to worry about. All is for the best. Noa will be here soon."

"Noah, as in the ark?"

"No, Noa as in your new mother-in-law."

"That was quick, Dad."

"Not by my standards, son. We have known each other for over a year."

"Biblically?"

"Not till recently. She is an Israeli PhD student."

"How Old Testament of you," I said with a grin.

"It's a new me."

"Clearly."

And with that I closed my eyes again and slipped back into a dream. Unfortunately, Egon had replaced the nun.

❧

Sometime later (it may have been days), I reemerged to find my friend the nurse changing my bedpan again. She maintained a safe distance. She needn't have worried. I was only supine this time.

As she squeaked back out, I noticed a figure sitting near

the end of the bed. On further inspection I saw that it was quite clearly Cherry, with a swaddled figure at her breast. She looked fantastic. A huge swell of love washed over me.

"Hi, honey," I said.

"Daddy!" she cried happily, lifting her head. The baby started crying less happily. She reattached it and stood up. "It's time for you to meet your daughter. We are so happy you are alive. I can't believe it really. Everyone here thinks you should have died."

"Sorry to disappoint," I smirked.

"You're so funny."

"Thanks."

"Now, you should know one thing," she said a little sheepishly.

"What?"

"She looks a little different than you might expect."

"How? Is she okay?"

"Oh yes, she's fine. Giving this pork queen no trouble at all. She's a doll."

My mind flashed back to the American Girl doll with the blue eyes and blonde hair. I couldn't wait to see her, despite Cherry's forewarning. My little baby girl.

"She's black, Cherry" was the only thing I could think to say as she held the baby out for me to take a look. It was a surprise, that's all.

"Half-black," Cherry corrected. "But don't worry, DeShaun has signed the papers. You just need to fill out a form and she can be all ours alone."

"DeShaun?" I managed to gasp out through the shock.

"I'm so, so sorry, baby. It was only once. Or twice. You were busy with other things. I don't know how it happened.

I only meant to give him a hummer, but one thing led to another. You know how open our relationship was."

"I do," I confessed. "Though I don't think babies were part of the arrangement. And I thought we were moving beyond that phase."

"We have! But this was before that. It seems like years ago."

"It was nine months ago."

"Right. And it won't ever happen again. But you have to promise me too."

"Of course I will," I offered magnanimously. I didn't really know what to think or do at that moment. My mind was still fuzzy, and now even fuzzier. She laid the little girl on my chest, and I have to admit it. It was love at first sight. She was more beautiful than I could possibly have imagined. I was so happy that I started crying. "Are you sure DeShaun doesn't want her?"

"Definitely. He's signed her away, like I said. He wants her to have a good home and a good life. He knows that he can't give her that, and he knows that you will totally love her."

"What a great guy," I said, only partially sarcastically. Near-death doesn't change us completely, it seems.

"I knew you would understand," she said, ignoring my tone.

"Of course I do," I said genuinely. "She's ours, and that's what matters, and I want us to be the happiest little family there ever was. Hey, maybe we can work on one of our own when I can move my legs again."

"You betcha. You're totally intact. The nurse tells me you aren't going to have any trouble in that area, and I've seen it with my own eyes." She smiled her cherry lips and wrinkled the tip of her perfect nose. I felt a surge of lust.

"It's ready and waiting," I said.

"Yup, that's apparent," she said, looking down at the tent I had made with the sheets. "But I think we'd probably better wait till we are alone. It feels a little wrong like with our baby right here. I don't want her getting all messed up."

"I'm not sure she will remember."

"You know, you're right," she said. And with that she manually eased my tension, as I cradled DeShaun's baby. Yes, it was odd. But I'm a man and I love my wife. What can I say?

CATASTROPHE(S)

I WAS WELL into my first few days of physical therapy when the doctors decided I was strong enough to be told the news. I'd been cut off from the outside world till then, which was fine by me, as I really couldn't have cared less what was happening anywhere beyond the hospital.

Holton was the man to do it, apparently.

"All gone," he said somberly.

"What do you mean?"

"Peter, POS, Zyxview, Egon, the last five years of stock market gains, all gone."

"Explain," I demanded as we sipped coffees in the day room.

"It's a long story."

"I'm not going anywhere fast."

Holton nodded. "Well, when you crashed in Egon's helicopter, the news hit the wires the next morning. I'll admit, I was so stunned that I passed the machinery in my rectum while talking to Peter. It took me a while to stuff it back in later in the gents."

"Unnecessary level of detail, Holton. Just the relevant points please."

"Okay, bro. Got it. Well, it's somewhat relevant in that we

lost the audio of Peter confessing everything to me. But the Feds had plenty of information already, so it wasn't a big deal."

"What are you talking about? For fuck's sake, Holton, spit it out." It was the first time I'd cursed since the crash, so knew I was getting better.

"Peter had been running a Ponzi scheme for years, taking cash from investors and spending it on himself while paying redemptions out of new investor money."

"Isn't that industry standard?" I half joked.

"Well, maybe," said Holton, thinking aloud. "But not quite as blatantly as that. Most fund managers at least pretend to invest the money."

"You mean he didn't invest it?"

"Not really. I mean he invested some. He invested in Zyxview, for example. It was gambling more than anything, hoping to make huge returns to pay off what he was taking out to buy all his houses, planes, cars, ex-wives, etc. The problem was he sucked."

"Not with Zyxview."

"No, he made a bit on Zyxview. Not as much as you'd think though. He'd only sold a small portion of his options when the stock went to zero. The rest were worthless."

"The stock is at zero?"

"Wow, you really don't know anything, do you?"

"I've been focused on other things. Like becoming a dad, trying to move my legs, and learning to eat again. The people here just kept telling me that everything was fine in the world. I guess they didn't want to worry me."

"You've got nothing to worry about. Except for finding a new job."

"POS is gone?"

"Exactly. When Zyxview fell to zero, the Feds moved in.

Peter clung to his Bloomberg screens and had to be physically dragged out of the office."

"What was the atmosphere like?"

"A mixture of elation at seeing the bastard get a taste of his own medicine, and total despondency that the whole game was over. Some were cheering, most were crying. Everyone was updating their LinkedIn profiles. They shut the office down a couple of days later. No one has been back since. There is a mirror sculpture going for next to nothing if you've got some free cash," he chortled.

"What happened to Zyxview, then?" I asked eagerly, trying to piece the puzzle together.

"Gone. When Egon died the stock fell eighty percent. Everyone downgraded it. Cramer went bearish. Then the SEC moved in, claiming they'd been about to pounce anyway. It turns out everything Egon said was bullshit. He didn't have any products. He didn't really have any concepts even. Everyone in the company thought everyone else had been working on things. Most of them had just been surfing porn at work it turns out."

"Like the federal government then," I commented.

"Pretty much. And so the stock went to zero in a matter of days."

"But what about The Peach?"

"What's The Peach?"

"The thing I crashed in, Holton."

"You crashed in Egon's helicopter, dude. Not that there was much left of it. I've been meaning to ask you what the fuck you were doing in a helicopter in the middle of the night in the Nevada desert."

It suddenly became clear. No one knew about The Peach. The mangled wreckage must have looked like any other helicopter crash. No one knew that Egon was only a partial fraud—that he had died on board the biggest revolution in transportation since the automobile. I decided that now wasn't the right time to clarify. "Oh, I guess he just called his helicopter The Peach. He loved it. He was taking me on a spin."

"More like a nosedive."

"I guess so. He was a crazy son of a bitch. Flew me out there just to take me on a ride. Said he had something to tell me."

"Did he?"

"Did he what?"

"Tell you anything."

"Only that he loved me."

"You're funny, dude," said Holton with a smirk. "Even after everything you've been through, you can still see the bright side."

"You betcha," I said, channeling Cherry. "There are more important things in life than money and power."

"Yeah, I've kind of realized that. The system is broken. But so what? If you don't care about the system, you don't need to worry about it."

"Right. It's possible the masses have gotten it right. Bread, circuses, and not giving a shit."

"Definitely."

"So where's Peter now?" I asked, hoping to hear he was locked up in some dingy cell, with only Bubba to keep him company.

"Dead," said Holton.

Shit, I couldn't even speak ill of him now. "What the fuck, did someone pop the poor bastard in jail?"

"Nah. Daria did it. He was released on bail, secured

against his castle. When Daria realized he was going to be worthless, she did the only thing an abused mail-order bride can do, and poisoned him. They found him lying face down on a rack in his dungeon, bloody lash marks all over his back. She went the extra mile. At least that's the rumor."

"Good on her," I said approvingly. "Still, no one deserves that fate."

"Bullshit," said Holton.

"I never speak ill of the dead," I replied.

"Fair enough. But he deserved worse."

"True."

"And now she's in jail and likely to go away for life."

"What a happy ending," I mused. "And I guess that leaves us high and dry."

"Well, I've stashed enough away to retire comfortably, albeit in North Dakota. I'm looking forward to getting away from this city. It's full of sociopaths, addicts, and narcissists."

"Only in high society," I corrected.

"Yup. I'm going to join low society. Do a real job. Use my hands. Get to meet normal human beings who care about things that matter."

"Don't get too excited. They're probably more abnormal than you realize."

"Normally abnormal."

"Exactly."

AURORA EX MACHINA

I'M SITTING HERE writing this all down as I gaze out over our farm in Iowa. It's an idyll—hog heaven, as Cherry and her mom would call it. Out of one pane of glass there's a ram humping a ewe, and out of another two farm boys shifting manure onto a truck. I'll probably go out later and walk the beans. What more could a man want out of life?

My ewe is downstairs making breakfast, and my (and DeShaun's) little lamb is fast asleep in the crib behind me. That's especially special, as the little terrorist has deprived me of most of my nighttime rest for the last six months. But I wouldn't want her any other way than she is. Nor would her grandma, grandpa, or the rest of town, it would seem.

We officially bought Cherry's mom's farm several months ago. She lives with us and couldn't be happier. My dad and Noa have visited us twice. He's a changed man, mostly.

In fact, it turns out that one of the reasons that my turkey trust fund had been depleted over time is that Dad had instructed the advisor to take out expensive insurance against a massive market crash. The guy thought he was an idiot, but, like all independent trustees, did exactly what he was told. When Zyxview crashed it brought down the whole market with it. The value of the fund trebled. My father is clearly a better investor than I am too. Still, I like to think that I contributed to that outcome in my own peculiar way.

We are now invested in yield, so have plenty to live off with relative security. Life in Iowa doesn't cost a fortune, which is interesting, as it's a darn sight better than a billionaire's life in New York. I guess some people just can't see outside their box. Perhaps they just enjoy the battle. Psychotic neurotics, every last one of them.

Holton saw the light, as you heard. He has also come to visit with his family a few times. It's only a nine-hour drive, which is next to nothing when you're out here. We laugh about the POS days and compare herds. I told him I had inside information on a new strain of corn. He politely declined to hear me out. His family is as gregarious and athletic as he is. His son could probably become an asset allocator if he doesn't get to the cheerleaders first.

Tom came out a month or so ago. Apparently, Fin re-entered their short position in Zyxview after the secondary. They also bought a lot of deep out-of-the-money puts for "extra juice," as he put it. Their hard work paid off and they'd made a fortune. Asset allocators were throwing money at them, and he had almost made enough to buy a two-bedroom house in Palo Alto. I congratulated him, and didn't bother mentioning he could buy half of Iowa for that. He seemed a bit bemused by my new take on life. I guess some people take a little longer on the Road to Damascus, but I know he'll come around. He's far too good a guy to keep doing what he's doing forever. I wished him luck with his new short, a Chinese company that claims to have solved the need for protein. I have a vested interest in seeing it fail, to be fair.

So, you may wonder, if you've made it this far, what impelled me to write all this down? Well, for one, I've been pretty bored. No one trusts me yet to do much on the farm, though I'm learning step by step, a couple of hours a day. Cherry says she thinks I'm a natural. But she's just being nice, as always. And she's got the baby covered most of the time. We named her Jill, by the way, after me, though I'll let you in on a little secret. My full name is Publius Vergilius Goodenough, Giles for short. Father thought it worth breaking the hereditary nomenclature in favor of the greatest poet of them all. We didn't saddle her with that. Jill Cheryl Goodenough suits her perfectly. Let's hope she's a lucky Jill too.

Speaking of which, the proximate cause of this ham-fisted attempt at a memoir turned up on my doorstep a few days after Tom left. She was a beautiful middle-aged lady, dressed in neat business casual attire, and in her hand she carried a lockbox. I took it and thanked her. For what I didn't yet know.

"The code is three-two-one," she said as she headed back toward the pickup she had come in. "He wanted you to have it. You own it now."

"Own what?" I asked in surprise. She didn't reply. "Who are you?" I shouted as she began to back out.

She rolled down the window. "Dawn. Don't you recognize me?" She laughed at my obvious bewilderment. "Good to see you again, Giles." And with that she drove off into the setting sun.

"Who was that hottie?" asked Cherry when I came back inside.

"She works for an administrator. She brought me something I left in Peter's office."

"Well, isn't that nice of them. I'd have totally thought they would have kept it. That's a long way for them to come."

"I know. And I still fear administrators, even when they bring me gifts."

"Quite right. Well, let me know what's inside. I'm going to go finish the Maid-Rites for us, then it's time to wake up little Jill for her lunch. How did the milking go this morning?"

"Udderly terribly."

"You're so funny." She giggled. Apparently, my transition from husband jokes to dad jokes was going smoothly.

I went upstairs and opened the box carefully. I admit that I was puckering. I just didn't think there could be any good news in anything that linked me to Egon.

I was wrong.

Inside, on ten memory sticks, were all the patents, designs, specifications, components, and manufacturing instructions that made up The Peach. There were legal documents that appeared to transfer ownership of everything to me upon Egon's death. And there was even a little note inside a blank envelope.

"To Giles. Love Egon. All is for the best."

THE END

Made in the USA
Coppell, TX
30 October 2020

40385912R00118